ARKANSAS HEAT

VOLUME TWO

A BRUTHA'S OBSESSION

BY

KAREN MARIE COLEMAN

COPYRIGHT © 2013 Karen Marie Coleman

ISBN-13: 978-1-7328314-4-5

Website- www.karencoleman.org

TABLE OF CONTENTS

CHAPTER ONE

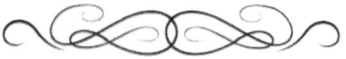

Chad Lancaster was on his way to the airport to pick up his brother Nigel. In Miami, on business, he took time out of his busy schedule to do so. He began nervously tapping the steering wheel as he was nearing his exit. He was having feelings of regret for agreeing to his brother's visit. Having him in town would be a major inconvenience, but as a favor to his mother, he agreed to let him stay. She worries about Nigel and feels that Chad would be a positive influence on him and possibly help keep him out of trouble.

Nigel often made poor choices, which resulted in Chad rescuing him. Whether it's helping him pay off bookies and bad debts or rescuing him in bar fights, he's always there for him. Nigel loved to play more than work, and he wasn't as devoted to his business as his brother. He was on the verge of losing a multi-million-dollar company until his brother stepped in and put up the money to save it.

Chad and Nigel are identical twins. Nigel was born four minutes after his brother. Soon after his birth, complications arose, resulting in long-term health problems. The family often spent many nights in the emergency room. When they were younger, Chad took it upon himself to help with Nigel whenever he was sick. Nigel's health issues subsided around age seventeen. He was older; however, he wasn't any wiser. He was getting into trouble in high school and at college, engaging in childish pranks. Since he was a star basketball player, the coaches protected him. He'd grown accustomed to everyone coddling him. He was never forced to deal with the ramifications of his actions, resulting in selfish and arrogant behavior. He only cared about himself and his needs. He lived for the moment and rarely thought his actions through.

Again, Nigel's actions have caused him trouble, and he needs to be rescued by his brother, who is forced to drop everything to accommodate him, and his timing couldn't be worse. Although Chad's company headquarters, Chadwick Designs, was based in his hometown of Little Rock, Arkansas, he conducts most of his business in Miami at his private marina. He designs luxury yachts and sailboats for high-end clients. He also designs luxury motor coaches. He's highly sought after for his ability to create impeccable one-of-a-kind designs, and his clients were more than willing to go on a two-year waiting list in to have him design their products. His creative designs with his signature logo were more about prestige. Because of his meticulous eye for the tiniest detail and his talent, it creates time constraints, thereby allowing him to do only a select few. The resale value of his brand is significantly higher once complete. What started as a hobby turned into a lucrative source of income. In addition to designs, another part of his business was repairs, boat charter services, and boat sales. His marina has a small restaurant on site. He was busy with clients and swamped with work, and he didn't need his bothersome brother in his way. As he made his way onto Miad Circle, his cell phone rang. It was his mother.

"Hello, mother."

"Hello, son. Has your brother's plane landed?"

"His plane is supposed to be landing at two o'clock; it's only one forty-five. He still must get off the plane and get his luggage. I'm pulling up at the airport now."

"Okay, I was just checking on him. Have him give me a call. I just want to know he landed safely."

"Okay, Mom, I'll have him call." Chad ended the call with his mother. *"That woman worries way too much."*

Fifteen minutes had passed, and he began to think of all he had to do for the day. His thoughts were interrupted by Amanda, his assistant.

"Chad, will you be able to make your four o'clock meeting?"

"Yes, let them know the meeting will start on time."

"I sure hope so. This is the Kensington family, and we don't want to disappoint them. They've been on the waiting list for a while now, and you don't want to lose them as clients. They're eager to meet with you, so hurry back."

"I'll be there on time Amanda."

Chad checked a few messages and made several more phone calls while waiting for his brother. Nigel walked up to the vehicle and began tapping the passenger side window, motioning for Chad to open the trunk. Chad glanced up from looking at his phone. He popped the lever to the trunk and got out to help with his bags. After they were done loading the trunk, they both got in the vehicle. Nigel said,

"Hey man, thanks for letting me hang out at your crib. Man, I had to get away from Arkansas for a while. Those country ass hoes were driving me crazy; a bunch of fucking stalkers are what they are. You can't put dick in any of those bitches without them acting a fool because they can't handle that shit. Bitch burned down my fucking house. I mean, can you believe that shit?" Chad said,

"That's because you're not honest with them. You can't play games with women and expect them not to respond. Are you crazy? First, you flatter them, take them on expensive dates, and then tell them you're interested in a long-term relationship. You tell them all the things they want to hear, and after you sleep with them a few times, you break it off with no warning." His brother, sounding proud of himself, said with a cheesy grin,

"Man, bitches believe that shit too. They eat it up with their gullible asses!" Chad looked at him and said,

"And that's why ole girl's got *you* running like a little bitch." Looking embarrassed with a partially bruised ego, Nigel said,

"Man, ain't nobody got me running like no bitch. I'm just taking a mini-vacation here until the insurance company straightens things out for me." Chad looked at him with a slight smirk, knowing he was too embarrassed to admit the truth said,

"Nigel, you have two other homes; why didn't you stay in one of them?"

"Because that crazy bitch is still on the loose! I ain't going back to Arkansas until the police catch her psychotic ass. She knows where all my spots are. I screwed her in all of'em. Do you think I'm going to hang out like a sitting duck and let her burn my ass up? Hell no. Besides, I thought I'd come out here to Miami and check out some of these big-booty, fine-ass women out here. I hear they don't be tripping like those Arkansas women. You know I must have a variety of ladies; I'm not like you. You're looking for somebody to wife. You're a one-woman man. I need options." He continued talking while Chad shook his head.

"You're down here in Miami with some of the finest women, and you're still not getting any action. I don't know why. I mean, you're a good-looking man. I know that because I am. Shit, we're identical, but still, I get more action than you."

Chad glanced at him and said,

"You may be getting more action, but you've got more problems, and anyway, those Arkansas sisters aren't tripping. Have you ever thought that maybe it's you? I happen to know a lot of beautiful women back home. Our mother is an Arkansan. They're good women, but they don't like taking shit from guys, especially if the guy's an asshole."

"Man, why I gotta be an asshole?"

"I'm not saying you're an asshole, but if the shoe fits, lace it up and wear it proudly. Stop calling them bitches and whores. Address them correctly. All you have to do is treat the ladies right, and they'll do the same. I have a lot of good women on my team back home. Besides, I date often, but I don't advertise it as much as you do. I'm honest with myself and with my dates. I'm a very busy man, and I travel often. I don't have the time it takes to be in a relationship. I let my dates know up front so they won't get their feelings involved. They're very understanding."

Nigel shook off what his brother was saying. "Whatever, man, I haven't seen you with a woman in almost a year. I can't believe you're letting all of this good pussy pass you by." Nigel spotted a few women in the airport parking lot. "Man, look at that over there. I haven't been here five minutes and already I see some fine-ass females. Wow, look at her, ain't she fine? Oh damn, look at the sitter on that critter over there! Ooh wee, man, I'm going to love hanging out in Miami."

Chad expressed to him that his visit should only be temporary and that he should keep his focus on why he was there.

"Who's going to run your company while you're in Miami?"

"Chad, man you know that place practically runs itself. I sit back and collect the money."

Nigel started his business fresh out of college. He named it Lancaster Logistics. His company conducts business in all fifty states, with several warehouses in each state. The business grew faster than expected, and soon after making his first few million, Nigel began to neglect his responsibilities by partying. He relied heavily upon his employees, who were not qualified to run a business that size. His trucks were barely street legal, leading to many repairs; his warehouses were becoming so outdated that it was creating hazardous conditions for the employees, and equipment failures were on the rise. He was on the brink of losing the company. Other corporations had planned on taking advantage of the company's sliding sales and buying it dirt cheap, but Chad stepped in and put up the money needed to keep it afloat. He worked there for a while, putting his own business on hold for about a year. He purchased new equipment, poured a ton of money into repairs, and renovated the warehouses. He also purchased a new fleet of trucks. He appointed qualified personnel to key positions to oversee the day-to-day operations. He hired a special liaison he could trust to monitor the company to ensure its success. The liaison was told to report directly to Chad while also keeping Nigel informed. This is one of the many ways he helped his brother, knowing he was immature and lacked any real commitment, by opting to play instead of putting in the extra effort to make his business thrive.

"You need to give mom a call and let her know you made it. You know she's going to be worried about you until she hears from you," Chad said.

"I'll call her later. She'll be okay. I can't wait to get to the condo, get me a drink, and find me a little something to play with."

"About that, I don't want a bunch of strange women in my condo, Nigel. I'm serious this time."

"Oh man, don't start with that. Where else am I going to take them?"

"How about taking them to a hotel?"

"Why would I do that?"

"Man, I'm not playing. I don't want them in my place. Get a room if you want to party or rent your own condo. Miami has plenty to choose from. You have the money."

"Man, you're no fun at all. You need to join me, let me hook you up with your square ass. I can show you a few pointers."

"I'll pass on that. My condo is not for your private sex parties. I take my clients there, and it's where I rest. I've invested too much time and money into my home, and I don't want a lot of trashy, naked females lying all over my furniture while getting drunk in my place. I don't do it, and I don't want you to do it either."

Nigel scoffed, "I don't know why you got that fancy-ass place anyway if you don't want anyone else to use it. Don't worry, I won't bring anyone to your place. At least you can let me use one of the boats since you won't let me party at your crib."

"We'll see," Chad said. He felt the compromise was far better than allowing his brother to have his way at his home, especially since he'd poured several million dollars into his condo alone and was very particular about it. He owned many boats, so allowing his brother to have access to either of them was fine with him. He loved seeing his family enjoy the fruits of his labor, especially his brother, but he always knew that Nigel bears watching as he had the propensity to act immaturely.

"Perhaps I can make that happen, but I need you to stay out of the way, don't cause any trouble down at the marina, and don't be bossing my employees around. You will take whatever vessel is available at the time. Don't ask for special favors because my clients have booked those boats in advance. If you can behave yourself, then I'll allow it, but if you fuck it up, it's over, and you know it. Oh, and one more thing: please don't sexually harass the female staff. I care about my employees and don't want any legal issues.

"Why do you always tell me that like it's a disclaimer or something? You're talking to me like I'm a child. I'm still a grown man last I checked. You know I'll never do anything to compromise your business."

Although Chad was an over-protective brother, Nigel knew that when it came to Chad's business, all bullshit took a back seat, and he respected the boundaries put in place by his brother. He was very strict with Nigel, or anyone for that matter, who would dare to interfere with his brand.

"Oh, I know you won't," Chad said, looking at him sternly. Nigel wanted to change the subject. He knew just discussing the matter was irking Chad's nerves, so he said,

"Relax bro, I'll be cool. I just thought perhaps I could charter a boat with a few beautiful ladies since I'll be in town indefinitely. If not, I'll rent a vessel from another marina and stay out of your way. Anyway, you just be ready for me to whip your ass in a game of pool tonight."

"No sir. I'm still the reigning champ, so you get ready to pay up." They talked more about their plans until they made it to Chad's condo. He gave Nigel his key card.

"They're waiting for you. They know you're coming. Some of them might mistake you for me but I informed the staff that you would be arriving without me. Ask for Alfie; he'll take care of all your needs."

"Thanks again, bro," Nigel said. The doorman helped him with his luggage, and Chad pulled away to go to his meeting.

Chad pulled up to the marina. He noticed a white, late-model Rolls Royce parked sideways in the parking lot. The driver was standing at the vehicle's side door, dressed in a suit and tie. He had his hands perfectly folded down in front as he was anticipating his passenger's return. Chad was anxious to get inside. He didn't want his clients to have to wait a second longer than needed. His office assistant, Amanda was pacifying them until he got there. He walked hurriedly into the meeting room, where he noticed a beautiful, well-dressed, elderly Hispanic woman draped in large, expensive jewelry. Standing to the right of her was a younger, even more beautiful version of her.

Chad fixed his eyes on the younger lady. He tried not to stare, but he couldn't seem to help himself. He was mesmerized. Her long flowing, dark brown hair partially covered one of her big brown eyes as she peeped up at him. Her golden honey-brown skin was smooth as silk and appeared perfectly tanned, partly from the Miami sun and her Hispanic heritage. She wore a teal mini-skirt that fit snugly against her petite but very shapely figure. Chad had seen plenty of pictures of her from various media

14

sources, but she was even more beautiful in person. As he looked on, he thought the former images of her were deceiving at best, as they never captured the true beauty of such an elegant and classy lady.

Her father is Herbert Kensington, a major player in the oil industry, and a well-respected, powerful man in the world of finance. Chad is used to working with wealthy clients, but he was a bit nervous about this one; not so much nervous as he was curious. The wife and the daughter of one of the wealthiest men in the south had personally come to visit with him. It was told that the daughter was eager to meet him. It's customary for someone with financial means to send a liaison to handle their business affairs, but these clients chose to handle this project themselves. As always, when it comes down to his business, Chad was always on his game. Although he was on time, he apologized to them anyway. He would've preferred to have been in the conference room waiting for them rather than the other way around.

"Hello, ladies; I must apologize for my tardiness. I had an important matter that needed my immediate attention." The younger lady said,

"It's okay; we're just glad to meet the fabulous Mr. Chad Lancaster of Chadwick Designs finally."

Chad was handsome. His naturally fine hair was a bit curly, which he kept professionally cut in a style that accented his strong, rugged facial features. He had a smooth, deep-brown complexion with a slight muscular build. Not the grotesque body type. Everything was in the right place, and his tailor-made suit fit him perfectly. His designer shoes were polished to perfection, and he smelled great. He made his way over to both ladies and shook their hands. The younger lady gladly gave him her hand. "I'm Blaire Kensington, and this is my mother, Elaine." The subtle hint of his cologne wafted across her nostrils, causing an instant tingling sensation between her legs. She looked at him intently, wanting his eyes to lock on hers. Just as she'd hoped, they did. He flashed a warm gentle smile. *"Shit, I bet he's great in bed,"* she thought. She allowed her hand to linger in his.

"It's a pleasure to meet you. May I offer you something to drink?" Both ladies declined the offer. Blaire regained her composure and began to speak.

"As I told your assistant, Father will be celebrating his sixty-seventh birthday in nine months, and we want to have his yacht renovated as a surprise for him. He won't hear of changing boats. He says *"The Elaine"* is his good luck charm. It's a little outdated, and we know you're the best, so here we are."

"Thank you, Mrs. Kensington," he said. She quickly corrected him.

"It's *Ms.* Kensington; my mother is Mrs. Kensington. I'm not married." His lips curved upwards into an apologetic smile at the admission of her single status.

"I apologize, *Ms.* Kensington." There was temporary silence as the two gazed at each other. He studied her eyes for a moment. She flashed a coy smile, leaving him in awe. He came to himself and cleared his throat. He didn't want to waste any more of their time, so he proceeded with the meeting.

"I've taken the liberty to draw up plans for your father's boat from the pictures we took while there. I have some amazing ideas that I'm sure you would love, and that your father will enjoy for years to come. Amanda has the slides ready for the presentation."

While his assistant was starting the video, Chad helped both ladies with their seats, first the elder and then her daughter. The younger smiled as he gently pushed her seat under her. He walked over to take a seat himself.

"Take a look at the screen. Here are a few ideas that I've constructed from the assessment interview. I would love for you to explain to me in detail where you would like to go from here. I want to modernize some of the spaces while keeping some elements of the design masculine. We'll gut the galley and produce an entirely new space. Any chef would be proud to use this space with new appliances in this top-of-the-line, state-of-the-art kitchen. Also, the vessel will need some minor repairs, but that won't be a problem. For the most part, the engine is up to par. I do, however, want to bring everything up to code. We handle all of that here on-site. When we're finished with this vessel, you won't recognize her." They were pleasantly surprised and excited about the designs.

17

"Oh, my goodness, this is amazing! Daddy's going to be pleased," Blaire said. "Mom, look, isn't this lovely? It hardly looks like the same boat." Her mother gently clasped her hands together. With a beaming smile, she said,

"Honey's going to love it?"

They continued the meeting which lasted about an hour making only minor changes as they went. After wrapping things up, he thanked them both., which lasted about an hour,

"If you need me or if you would like to discuss the plans further, I'm always a phone call away," Chad said while handing Mrs. Kensington his card. Her daughter intercepted it. Gazing into his eyes flirtingly, she said,

"We'll be in touch." He escorted them out to the lobby. Afterward, he went back to the meeting room where Amanda was putting things away and turning off the video.

She looked up at him and asked, "Well, what are your thoughts about the Kensingtons?"

"I think the meeting went very well." With pursed lips, she looked at her boss and said,

"I didn't ask you about the meeting; I asked you about the Kensingtons."

"What do you mean? I thought they were very nice. They both seemed very happy with the new designs."

She interrupted him and said, "*Ms.* Kensington was a little *too* excited, don't you think?"

"No, she was just happy to get the designs she wanted," Chad said as he was putting his things in his briefcase. Amanda looked at him and said sarcastically,

"I'm so sure. The designs weren't the only thing she was interested in. I noticed her admiring you."

With a look of confusion, he said, "What? No, I don't think so; what makes you say that?"

"Chad, that woman was flirting with you throughout the entire meeting."

"I hadn't noticed. I thought she was nice and very friendly."

"Chad, you never seem to notice when women are coming on to you. I've seen it for years, but you're always working too hard or too worried about that brother of yours to notice. She likes you. The heiress to the Kensington throne was sitting right here in your office flirting with you and you never even noticed. Do you know how many men's hearts would skip a beat if she looked their way? Yet there you sat nonchalantly without a clue." He loosened his tie a little and took a seat.

"Well, if it's any consolation, my heart skipped a beat when I walked into the room and saw her in person for the first time. She's a beautiful lady."

"She's also very eligible. She hasn't been seen with anyone since that nasty break-up where her ex-boyfriend actor Bradley Abbott, was caught with the actress he starred in that last movie with. What's her name? Was it Sonja Evans or something like that? She had since flown under the radar. Poor girl must live her life in the public eye. I think she left and went to some private island for a while, as the press said, to *heal and to reflect*." It looks as if she's healed and she has her eyes on you."

"Stop saying that; you don't know that for sure." She looked at him with a sly smile that said, she knew something he didn't know.

"Okay, but don't say I didn't warn you." She gathered her things and left.

Chad leaned back in his chair and tried to replay the events of the meeting. He still couldn't see what Amanda saw. In his mind, the lady was only being friendly. He shook off the thought, went to his office, and began working on the Kensington project on his computer. While doing so, his phone rang, startling him. He picked it up on the first ring.

"Chadwick Designs." The voice on the other end was soft but confident.

"Hello, I would like to speak to Mr. Lancaster, please."

"This is Chad Lancaster how may I help you?"

"So, you answer your own phone, Mr. Lancaster?"

"Well, the business office is closed for the day. Everyone else has already gone home, including my receptionist and my assistant. I'm the only one here. To whom am I speaking?"

"This is Blaire Kensington. Mother and I were discussing the designs, and we wanted to add a few more details. I told her that I would handle it. I want to know if we could meet soon to discuss them, perhaps over dinner."

Chad hesitated for a second, briefly thinking about what Amanda said.

"Are you sure you would like to meet for dinner? I can always schedule an appointment for you here in the office. It'll probably be more convenient for you."

"No, I would love for you to have dinner with me," she said.

"Okay, if you insist. When would you like to meet?"

"How about tonight?"

"I apologize, but my brother and I have plans tonight. We'll be at the Billiard Room Lounge; he's in town, and I promised to take him. How about tomorrow? I don't have anything scheduled." She gladly accepted and said,

"That'll be great. I'll call you with the details."

They ended their call. Thinking about what Amanda said, he smiled and shook his head. He called his mother to check on her and went home to prepare for his pool game with Nigel.

The Billiard Room Lounge is one of Chad's favorite places to unwind and play his favorite game. The lounge was exclusive and catered to high-class wealthy lovers of the game. Membership is required to enter the premises, or a member must invite you. Chad has held his membership for four years. In addition to the game of billiards, members could enjoy a game of poker, chess, and many other activities. Along with the great food and cocktails, they offered some of the best cigars money could buy, from a cheap stogie to thousands for a single cigar. There were many blends and brands to choose from. They had an amazing smoking room and a built-in humidor.

Although it originally catered to men, they dropped that policy many years ago, and now everyone enjoys the lounge. More men than women still frequent the place. Chad and Nigel were great at playing pool, and they often played in tournaments when they were younger, winning several trophies. Now, they only play for fun. They entered the club's parking lot. The valet driver took Chad's vehicle, and they went inside. It was Nigel's first visit there. The entrance of the building had the traditional feel of old money with deep brown woods, and dark leather furniture. Still, as you entered into the action, there was more of a modern atmosphere created for the younger, wealthier members with new money gained from the tech industry and the new world of finance. It was quite impressive. Chad and Nigel got a couple of cigars. They were seated. Nigel looked over the lounge, saying,

"Man, this shit is nice. When you said we were going to play pool, I wasn't expecting all of this. Damn, I've been to many pool halls, but this place is like nothing I've been to before. This shit is for the elite motherfuckers." Feeling a little annoyed, Chad looked at him with a slight frown and said, "You know, Nigel, it's hard to believe that you and I were raised in the same home by the language you use. Sometimes you can be so ghetto."

In a sarcastic tone, Nigel looked at Chad and said, *"Well, gosh darn it, Mr. Lancaster. I apologize for my language here tonight. I'm sorry if I offended you."* He laughed.

Their hostess was a pretty redhead. She wore a tight black V-neck t-shirt with the company's logo on two pool cues. It seemed to barely cover her larger-than-average breasts. She also wore a short black server's skirt. After walking over to their table, she looked at the brothers. She was a bit confused. She was familiar with Chad because he was a regular customer. She wasn't aware he had a twin. They wore the same style of clothes, the same haircut, and even the same mustache and goatee. She couldn't tell which twin Chad was, so she addressed them both, "May I get you two gentlemen something to drink?"

Chad said, "I'll have bourbon."

Nigel was lustfully eyeing her body while smiling like the Cheshire cat. "Make that two, and I will have you on the side with your fine ass," Nigel made his remarks towards her in such a disrespectful manner that she could tell he wasn't Chad, who always treated her with respect. She flashed Nigel a smirk. She dropped two fresh ashtrays on the table and walked away.

Chad gave him a scolding look and said,

"Nigel, this isn't one of those cheap strip clubs you like visiting. Please be respectful of the ladies here. Don't insult them, and please don't come on to them with those cheesy pick-up lines. Sherry's a nice girl. Leave her alone and allow her to do her job without the harassing comments. She gets enough of that from these dirty old men." Taking a puff of his cigar, Nigel, true to form, said in an arrogant tone,

"Man, you're tripping. These bitches love me. I can get any woman I want. It's been working for me so far, so why stop now? I've never met a woman I couldn't fuck. Not one, even married women are all on my dick."

Chad interrupted him. "Oh man, not *the dick talk* again. Can you spare me tonight?" Nigel leaned back in his seat and began bragging,

"Well, aren't you proud of yours? Shit, I got the biggest dick in the South and the best tongue too. Once I get a hold of one of these females, they're hooked."

While Nigel was still talking, the young lady walked up with their drinks. She bent over, placing the drinks in front of them. While doing so, Nigel looked down her t-shirt. He wanted her to know he was looking at her breasts. She ignored him, focusing her attention on Chad. Chad gave her a hefty tip. He whispered in her ear,

"Thank you for everything. I apologize for my brother."

"Thank you, Mr. Lancaster." After she walked away, Nigel asked,

"What did you say to her?"

"I thanked her and apologized to her for your comment."

"Why did you do that? It was unnecessary. I'll make a bet with you. I bet you that I'll have her, in bed, by tomorrow morning."

"Nigel, you know I don't play those types of games."

Nigel left his seat while Chad was still speaking. He went over to the young lady. He whispered in her ear.

"Excuse me... Sherry, is it?" She nodded her head. "I'm sorry if I offended you. I really didn't mean to. I was so captivated by your beauty that I couldn't control myself. I know I was wrong. I get that way sometimes; it's the bad boy in me. Do you think there's any way that you could forgive me? If there's any way to make it up to you, I will."

She smiled and said, "No problem, sir." He reached into his pocket, pulled out a couple of hundred-dollar bills, and handed them to her.

"For any troubles I may have caused." He walked away. On his way back to his seat, she said,

"Sir, you didn't have to do that." He turned around and said,

"Yes, I did." After he baited the hook, they shared a quick chat. She gave him her number and went back to work. He went back to his seat. He dropped his phone on the table. With a cocky grin, he said,

"That's her phone number. I will be fucking that pussy tomorrow!" Chad shook his head. He took a sip of his drink.

Nigel looked up and noticed a lovely figure walking in the door.

"Damn! Look at this rich pussy coming up in here. Now that's going to be my wife in my next life."

Chad looked up and saw the beautiful woman walking in. She was dressed in the perfect little red dress. Although it was extremely short, it was very sexy and classy. Her long hair was perfectly displayed in the loveliest style, both sexy and glamorous, and her makeup was flawless. It was Blaire Kensington. Nigel stood to his feet. For the very first time in his life, he was truly taken aback by a woman's beauty. He wanted this woman. He wanted to get to know her.

Chad said breathlessly, "Ms. Kensington!" Nigel looked toward Chad and asked, "Man, do you know her?"

"Yes, she's one of my clients."

Blaire's eyes briefly scanned the room as though she was looking for someone. Several men who had gathered around were competing for her attention. She proceeded to the bar and then took a seat. Nigel hurried to where she was sitting. Chad, not wanting any drama, quickly followed. As soon as Nigel began to introduce himself, she interrupted him, believing him to be Chad.

"Hello Mr. Lancaster. It's great to see you again." She gave Nigel her hand. He kissed it and said,

"The pleasure is all mine. You're one fine ass woman." She quickly withdrew her hand. At that very moment, Chad walked over and intercepted the awkward conversation.

"Hello Ms. Kensington." She was a little confused when she saw Chad and Nigel standing side by side.

"Twins! Wow, I didn't know and identical at that. I can't tell you guys apart!" Shocked at seeing the two of them, she couldn't stop staring. She was trying to discover a difference. From her initial encounter with Chad and knowing he was a gentleman; she could tell the difference between the two by Nigel's behavior.

Chad said, "I didn't know you were a member."

"I'm not. My father holds a membership. After you told me you were coming here, I decided to check it out."

"Please, come and sit with me," Nigel requested.

"I'm fine right here," she said, directing her attention towards Chad, hoping he would offer.

"Ms. Kensington, would you please join us at our table?"

She smiled and said, "It would be my pleasure."

He took her by the hand and helped her out of her seat. They made their way to their table. Nigel tried flattering her all evening, but she ignored him and focused on Chad instead. She was kind to Nigel, but she was put off by his annoying advances. In the beginning, Nigel and Chad played a few rounds of pool. As Chad won round after round, Blaire continued to cheer him on. Growing tired and being a sore loser, Nigel threw his pool cue on the table and walked away. He stood in the background, watching Blaire and his brother in envy. He watched as she and Chad played a few rounds of pool.

Each time Blaire would bend over, her already short dress would expose more of her thighs and backside, which caused every man in the lounge to look on. Nigel couldn't understand why one of the most beautiful women before him, playing pool while looking amazing, was ignoring him. Nigel wasn't used to that. He tried everything to gain her affection, but she wasn't impressed. She simply wasn't interested in him. He was insulted. He'd never had a problem getting women. Women fell at his feet without him giving much effort. This is one woman he truly wanted, and she wasn't turned on by him in the least. After playing a few pool games and having a few more drinks, Blaire left reluctantly but not before confirming her dinner plans with Chad. After she left, Nigel drilled Chad about her.

"Man, you've got to hook me up with her. Put in a good word for me."

"Nigel, she's a wonderful lady who is totally out of your league. What am I supposed to say to her on your behalf? You're a player? Her interests are different from yours. Besides, she's my client, and I don't need any conflicts."

"Man, she's a woman. What other interests could she have besides a fine-ass brutha like me and some good dick? I want her Chad. Hook me up."

"Nigel, you were sitting right here with her. If she wanted you, she would've mentioned it. You came on to her all night, but she wasn't into you. You really have no clue, do you? You must be more in tune with a lady's needs. You came on too strong. Most women of substance hate that about a guy, and money and sex don't impress a real lady. You must come with more than that. She's already rich so what can you offer her other than money?"

Nigel shook off his brother's comment. He continued to beg his brother, but Chad wasn't moved by his request. He knew it would be disastrous to hook him up with Blaire.

"Stick to what you know, baby brother. Don't interrupt this lady's life with your bullshit. You're not ready for a woman like her."

While Chad was speaking, Sherry, their hostess, came to the table to get them another drink. She smiled at them both and took their drink orders again. Nigel followed her to the bar.

"Hey sexy, come here." She walked up to him. "Shit, you smell good," he whispered,

"I bet your pussy tastes as sweet as a sun-kissed Georgia peach."

She smiled and asked, "Are you curious enough to find out?"

"I want to taste you," As he whispered in her ear, she was enamored by his soothing voice and handsome looks. Looking him over, she imagined him indulging in and devouring her pussy. It was going to be a long night. It made no sense to turn him down. She could get off and have a productive night, and as far as she knew, it could lead to something better, and she wouldn't have to work there anymore.

She said, "Let me get these drink orders and come follow me." She filled the orders and took them to her customers. She then took Nigel by the hand. She grabbed a set of keys from the bar and led him to the back of the club. This area was off-limits to everyone except employees. She locked the door behind them, and she rushed to unzip his pants. She pulled his stiff penis out from his pants and popped the head of it in her mouth. He leaned back on the desk as she continued to serve him. He reached down and fondled her large breasts. He gently pushed her off and took her to the floor. He lifted her short server's skirt, pulled her panties down, and buried his head between her thighs. She positioned her body so that she could suck his member as he continued to pleasure her. Afterwards, he fumbled around in his pocket and pulled out a strip of condoms. He frantically opened one and placed the condom on; then he lifted her body towards him, moved her to the desk, and quickly fucked her. After a few minutes, he guided her around and bent her over the desk, and then inserted himself inside her anal walls. Much to his delight, she was totally into it. She placed her hand behind her and opened herself to him for him to gain total access. He reached beneath and massaged her clitoris. By now, she was ready to cum. She bent over even further as he thrust his member deeper within. Biting her bottom lip, she pushed her body back to him as she reached her climax. He then placed himself inside of pussy and aggressively fucked her with his pants still around his ankles. With one final thrust, he pulled her body to his and pinned her there as he emptied his load. He smacked her bare ass and said,

"Damn girl, you got some good pussy. I love Miami! You sure know how to make a man feel welcome."

He kissed her on the lips. After freshening up in the washroom, he zipped his pants and went back to where his brother was seated. Chad was curious as to where he had been. He asked,

"Man, where were you?"

"I had to take care of a little business back there." Chad looked at him, a bit puzzled, and asked,

"What type of business?"

Still short of breath from the event that had previously taken place, Nigel proudly said,

"Remember when I told you I would have that little freak over there in the morning? Well, I was wrong; I just fucked the shit out of her tonight." Chad was disappointed with him.

"Nigel, we didn't come here for that. I can't take you anywhere without you getting into mischief. Couldn't you at least wait? Oh, never mind." Sherry came back over to the table with complimentary drinks. She smiled at Nigel and walked away.

"Man, she's a real freak. I'm gonna love it in Miami. I may never move back to Arkansas. Now all I need for you to do is hook me up with that bad ass client of yours, and I'll be set. Shit, I'd travel to give her this dick."

"Nigel, I'm warning you. Stay away from Ms. Kensington."

Chad didn't want Blaire Kensington to be his brother's next sexual conquest. He felt obligated to keep Nigel away from her at all costs. He knew that his brother wasn't deserving of such a high-class lady and was incapable of having a functional relationship with her. Given what she has been through in the past, he knew Nigel was bad for business, very bad indeed. Chad took a sip of his drink and looked at his brother. For the first time in his life, he was truly disgusted with him.

The Following Morning

Nigel slept in late, hung over from the night before. Chad was getting ready for his next meeting at the office. His brother's cell phone rang throughout the night, disturbing his sleep. He was feeling a tad bit annoyed about it. As he was about to walk out the door, his cell phone rang. It was his mother.

"Oh damn, it's Mom. Hello mother."

"Hello, Chad, you don't sound very happy to hear my voice this morning."

"Mother, I'm always happy to hear from you. You're my favorite girl."

She laughed and said, "Yeah tell your mother anything. I won't hold you long son. I have to go to the gym, and then Annette and I are going to brunch."

"Tell Mrs. Barnes I said hello, and you two ladies had better behave yourselves. I don't need you to get into any trouble. I hear how you two drive those men crazy at that health club. I need that to stop. Don't make me come down there and whip somebody about my mom," he said. She laughed at him.

"I can't help it if I'm still good-looking at my age." They both laughed. "I was calling to check on you and your brother. How are y'all doing over there?"

"Nigel is doing okay, annoying as usual but he's okay."

"I called him all day yesterday. He never got back with me."

"Perhaps he was taking a nap. I asked him to call you at the airport. He said he would. I assumed he had already."

"Well, as long as he's okay, I guess I'll be getting off of here. I don't want to be late for my aerobics class."

"Okay, Mom, I'll talk to you soon. Enjoy your day."

Chad made it to the office. As he walked in, Amanda was sitting at her desk smiling. A large bouquet of roses partially blocked her cute brown face.

"Hello Chad," she said with a beaming smile.

"Well, who sent you roses? He must be a special guy because you're smiling from ear to ear."

"Oh, these aren't for me, boss; they're for you."

"Oh, you brought me roses?"

"Now Chad, I've been your assistant for five years now, and I have yet to buy you a single rose. These are from *Ms.* Kensington. The card says, *"Thanks for last night."* You sure move fast for a man who doesn't know when a woman is flirting with him."

"It's not what you think, Ms. Nosey; get your mind out of the gutter." She looked at him curiously wanting to know more.

"So, tell me, I was right, wasn't I? She does like you, huh."

"No, I think she's just being nice and hoping that our company does a great job for her family. Which reminds me: Did you send for the fabrics that I requested?"

"Yes, I did," she said as she followed him into his office.

"Also, that teak wood they wanted. I need the guys to get on that since it's being imported. It could take up to six weeks to get that in alone."

"I'm on it, boss. What a way to change the subject," she said. She placed the roses on his desk and then she went to her office and did as she was told. Chad worked on a few designs until his clients arrived for their meeting. After he was finished, he decided to go home and rest a while until his dinner appointment with Blaire. When he made it home, Nigel was up watching television.

"Hey man, why are you home so early? I thought you would be at work all day."

"As you know by now, my work hours are flexible. I didn't have any more appointments today, so I'm going to get a little rest. I sure could use a nap since your phone rang through the night, disturbing my sleep. Since you're so worried about my workday, have you called your office to check on your business today?"

"Man, I told you that place can run without me."

"That's how you got into trouble the last time and I had to bail you out. I'm not going to keep putting money into your company so that you can allow it to fail again. Why don't you let me buy it from you until you can find what it is, you're passionate about?"

"Man, I'm good. The company is fine and it's making money hand over fist."

"Well know this baby bro; if it starts to fail again, you're on your own."

Nigel looked at him frowning. "Why are you worried about my business? You already got the money back that you invested and then some. If it fails, which it won't, you won't be out of one thin dime!"

Chad threw his hands up and walked into his bedroom. He didn't feel like arguing with his spoiled brat of a brother. He showered and took a quick nap. After his nap, he got dressed for dinner. He took his iPad with him believing he would possibly be working through dinner. He took one last look at himself in the mirror. He headed for the door.

"Where are you going?" Nigel asked.

"I have an important business dinner tonight."

"Un-huh, is it business or pleasure because you're dressed to impress tonight."

"It's strictly business Nigel."

Chad hurried for the door. He didn't want to be late. The elevator seemed to take forever. A small amount of anxiety began to set in. He didn't understand why. He'd attended many business dinners in the past, but this one seemed to make him a little nervous. He began thinking of what Amanda said about Blaire Kensington. Maybe she was interested in dating him. She showed up at the Billiard Room lounge unannounced; she sent him roses and now dinner. Was his head buried in the sand? Did she have a crush on him? For the first time, he began to think about it seriously. He hurried to the restaurant. He made it before she did, so the maître d escorted him to his table. A few minutes later she arrived. He noticed her immediately as she walked in. Her hair was in an updo, and she was wearing a lovely white lace mini-dress with a diamond necklace and earrings. She was carrying a silver clutch and wearing shoes to match. Not only had he noticed her, but everyone else in the place did as well.

She floated in like a breath of fresh air, a vision of loveliness bestowing her beauty upon all her admirers. The men smiled as she walked into the room while the women looked on in jealous amazement. The maître d escorted her to the table. Chad stood to his feet as she walked over. He held her chair as she took her seat. "Ms.

Kensington, you look magnificent." She looked up at him and smiled as he began to take his seat.

"Thank you, Mr. Lancaster." He was seated. He waited for her to take the lead.

"So, tell me, Mr. Lancaster, how was your day?"

"I had a great day. It wasn't quite as busy as usual. Not too many clients today. I just had one meeting. I worked on your father's designs. I have them here, so if there's anything you would like to go over, we can do that."

She admired him and couldn't stop staring at him. She looked at his hands, imagining them caressing her body. Her eyes fell on his lips, which looked delicious. She desperately wanted to kiss them.

"Mr. Lancaster, I have a confession to make; I didn't invite you to dinner for work. I invited you because I want to get to know you." He leaned back in his chair a bit and smiled. He was speechless.

"Ms. Kensington, I don't know what to say."

"Well, for starters, you can stop calling me Ms. Kensington. It's so formal and cold. Call me by my first name."

"Okay, Ms. Kens… I mean Blaire."

"May I call you Chad?"

"Yes, of course."

"Now that we've gotten all the formal stuff out of the way, we can finally relax. Are you currently dating anyone Chad?"

"I'm not seeing anybody exclusively if that's what you're asking."

She smiled when he answered. She knew he wasn't married, and she hoped he wasn't seeing anyone.

"Why hasn't anyone snatched you up by now? You seem like a real catch," she said.

"I have friends. I date at times, but honestly, I haven't had much time for dating or relationships, for that matter. Between running my company and traveling from several states, I'm never in one place for long. I don't want to put that type of strain on a lady. I think that a woman deserves more time than I can give. I've tried being in a serious relationship a couple of times, but it just hasn't worked for me. They wanted me home, but my work demands so much of my time. In the beginning, they say they can handle it, but as time goes on, eventually work wins out, and they leave. To tell you the truth, I can't blame them. What about you?"

"As you may have heard, I broke up with my ex-fiancé. After the breakup, I took some time for myself. I wanted to heal, and I didn't want to do it in the public eye. Before I dated my ex, my life was pretty much low-key. I was well known in my circle but when you date someone from the Hollywood scene, your private life is no longer private. The media can be so cruel and insensitive. They demand to know everything about your life. Intimate things that should never see the light of day. They report on your personal life regardless of your feelings. I think it's wrong. I wonder how they would feel if someone were to shine a light into their lives, especially during the dark moments. After things died down, I came back home and threw myself into my work. But I'm refreshed. I feel empowered, and I'm doing great. I'm not about to stop living or loving because of one heartbreak. My past hurts don't define me."

"Well put. I think you are an amazing lady. It's good to see you're doing so great. I saw the tabloid's stories. I remember thinking, *"Why don't they leave that poor lady alone?"* It was difficult to watch, but I must admit that you handled it with poise and grace. Now it looks like you're back and better than ever."

"I was always good. I just wanted to be alone. I knew the relationship wasn't good for me, but I was relieved when it ended. The media blew the whole thing out of proportion. It's hard to heal when the news stories are a constant reminder of your relationship. I was fine; the media wanted it to appear I was in deep mourning but on the contrary. I was sick of hearing about it. I went on about my life because I knew one day it would be old news and I could go back to living a normal life. Now, the media has all but died down. I see a few stories occasionally, but nothing like they used to be. It would've been cool of them to give just as much coverage to my cancer foundation as they did to my private life. But everyone loves to gossip and sensational journalism, if you can call it that."

Chad said, "Tell me more about your cancer foundation."

"I started my foundation here in Miami to bring awareness to helping find the cure for childhood cancer. I'm a volunteer for the children's hospital. I visit with the cancer patients there. I'm a big supporter, and that's what I spend my time doing. I love helping the children. They're so brave. My heart goes out to them. When I see one of their little faces and see all they must go through, my little problems seem so trivial."

"You're an awesome young lady. So, how long have you been involved in cancer awareness?"

"For about six years now. My good friend's daughter had leukemia. While visiting her in the hospital, I met so many families dealing with similar illnesses, some even worse than hers. Her little friend died while she was there, which just broke her little heart and ours too. I began meeting many families and lending a helping hand whenever possible. Some parents quit their jobs to care for their sick children full-time, and my foundation helps them with expenses while giving money for research. We're able to help thousands of families every year through donations that come in. My parents help too.

Dad has many business partners and friends who donate millions of dollars, and Father has the annual golf tournament in May for the charity. It's become a pretty big deal in my family. My parents are just as passionate about it as I am."

Chad smiled and said, "That sounds great. I would love to know more. You and your parents seem like wonderful people. I'm curious, Blaire, how did your parents meet?"

"My father is from Texas. My mother is from Mexico. My grandparents came here from Mexico to seek a better life for my mother. My grandmother worked for my grandfather. When my mother was younger, she would go to work with my grandmother, who sometimes helped her with her duties. She and my father began to hang out together. In their late teens, my father fell in love with my mother, and they began to date secretly. My grandparents disagreed with the relationship in the beginning. Neither side thought it was a good idea, but my father never wavered. The more they tried to keep them apart, the more they wanted to be together. When my grandparents realized he was determined to be with her, rather than lose their only son, they allowed them to date. They were hoping that it was just a phase. It wasn't, and their love is as strong today as it was in the beginning. I'm the product of that marriage."

The waiter came by with the wine list. They ordered wine, and then a few minutes later, they ordered dinner. Taking a sip from her glass, she looked at him and smiled. He noticed just how beautiful she was at that moment. Her eyes sparkled. He couldn't keep himself from staring. She was sweet and a bit flirty. *"What is her fascination with me? Out of all the eligible bachelors in this town, she has set her sights on me."* Her smile was lovely and contagious. He couldn't help but return a smile of his own. She was breaking him. For a minute, he felt that she could be the woman for him. He imagined her in his life. He shook himself and thought, *"What in the hell's wrong with me? I'd better get it together. It's only dinner."* She broke his train of thought.

"What's on your mind?"

Feeling embarrassed as if she could read his thoughts, he cleared his throat and said, "Oh, nothing"

"Do you want to know what's on my mind?"

"Sure, tell me."

I was just imagining you without your shirt." He laughed nervously and took a sip of his water.

"I'm just being honest," she said. "I hope I'm not making you uncomfortable. You look a little embarrassed."

He smiled and said, "You're fine. I'm not embarrassed."

"I apologize for being so forward, but I'm interested in getting to know you. Do you have a problem with that? By the way, I heard your little speech about not having time for a long-term relationship. Would you be interested in going out with me again?"

"Well, actually, I never thought about it before tonight. I was looking at this dinner from a business perspective. I want to do a great job for your family. I never expected this night would happen, even in my wildest dreams. I think that you're an amazing young lady. Any man would be lucky to have you.

You and I are from two different worlds. You were born into money. I'm a country boy from Arkansas. I come from a working-class family. My parents worked hard so my brother and I could attend great schools. The funny thing is; after graduating college, I didn't even work in my field of studies. My hobby has made me wealthy, but there were days when I wasn't sure how I was going to pay the bills. I was robbing Peter to pay Paul. You may not know the struggle of having to make decisions based on whether or not there would be enough money." She interrupted him,

"Let me stop you right there. I may not know what it's like to have financial struggles, but I'm human, and I've struggled with some, if not more, of the same issues that women across America have. Just because I have money doesn't mean that I can't relate to humanity. If you're going to turn me down, please don't do it based on that argument."

He apologized and said, "Looks like I stepped in it big time, huh? I wasn't trying to turn you down. Actually, I admire you too, and the thought of going out with you thrills me. While it's true I've amassed a great deal of wealth, it pales in comparison to the kind of wealth you're accustomed to. In addition to that, I know you've been through a lot and I don't want to add to your troubles with my busy life."

He could tell by the expression on her face that she wasn't moved by what he was saying. Realizing he was getting nowhere he asked,

"May I ask you a question?" She looked at him almost pouting and said,

"Go ahead."

"How about a do-over? Would you like to have dinner with me again?" She smiled.

"Of course, I would. I thought you'd never ask."

They both laughed. They enjoyed their evening together. After dinner, they went dancing at some of Miami's hottest nightclubs. He watched as she danced and laughed. She was no ordinary woman. She was fun, feisty, sexy, and beautiful. She was spicy, which turned him on. He knew being friends with her was going to be an enjoyable journey, and he was all in for the ride.

CHAPTER TWO

Three weeks had passed, and Chad and Blaire had already been on several dates. She was falling for him fast. She made a habit of calling him early in the morning and he looked forward to the morning calls. This morning was no exception.

"Good morning," she said.

"Good morning you."

He smiled instantly after hearing her voice.

"You know what I was thinking last night? I would love to come to your place and fix you dinner."

He smiled at the notion of her coming to his home, but then he thought about Nigel. Blaire was insisting on coming, and he didn't want to deny her request. He knew he had to get rid of his brother.

"I would be glad to have you over, but you don't have to cook for me."

"I insist. I would love to."

"I didn't know you could cook. So, you're a woman of many talents."

"Yes, I have my moments. What time may I come over?"

"How about six"

"See you soon."

Nigel overheard him talking on the phone. "Man, who's this new girl you're seeing?"

"Oh nobody." Chad never told Nigel that he was dating Blaire. It was none of his business.

"By the way, she's coming here tonight for dinner. Do you think you can find something to do for a while tonight?"

"Of course; this is Miami, and there's always something to do. I'm just happy to see you're finally getting some action."

"It's not like that, man."

"So, you ain't even hitting it yet?"

"Nigel, not everything is about sex. You can have plenty of fun enjoying one another's company through great conversation and finding pleasure in doing wonderful things together. You're not interested in women for anything other than your own sexual pleasure. You don't listen to them or talk to them. You talk to them long enough to get them in bed, and you're finished with them afterward. When you truly want a lady or a relationship, sex takes a back seat to all that bullshit you're doing."

"Man, I'm not ready for a serious relationship right now. I'm only interested in sex, so that's what I do. I don't need some woman hanging all over me all the time. Am I supposed to have only one woman? I mean, where's the fun in fucking the same woman over and over again? Shit, my dick would get bored."

"Nigel, I'm not trying to change you, but if you want to make your life less difficult, you may want to be honest with women and tell them that you're not interested in a relationship. Tell them that your relationship with them is strictly physical, and please, never let them know where you live because you'll need to increase your insurance premiums. They'll continue burning your homes, trashing your cars, and have you constantly on the run, that's if you don't get seriously hurt first."

"Bro, how many times do I have to tell you? I'm not on the run. I'm just laying low, that's all." Chad laughed.

"Nigel man, I need you to make yourself scarce before my date arrives. Miami has plenty of nice places to go, as you know. You can hire a driver to take you anywhere you want, or you can pick a place and put it in your GPS in the rental."

"I'll be alright, don't worry about me. Hell, I got this. Shit, I'm gonna pimp this fucking city. Miami won't be the same when I leave."

Nigel left the room while Chad got dressed for work. Chad could hardly wait for his date with Blaire. He rushed and got everything done for the day and hurried home. He purchased a large bouquet of assorted floral arrangements and had them delivered to his condo. He called ahead and had the concierge set up his dining area.

When he made it home, he noticed Nigel hadn't left. "Man, what time are you leaving? My date will be on her way in a few minutes."

"Hey, I'll be outta your hair. Can't you see I'm getting dressed?"

"Well, hurry up. I want this evening to be perfect."

"Damn bro, she's already got you wrapped around her finger, and you ain't even hit it yet. Chill, you're gonna be alright. Shit, I've never had to worry about impressing a woman because they're too intent on trying to impress me. If you ask me, I think you're doing too much. You're acting like this is the last piece of ass on earth."

Feeling a little agitated Chad said, "Well, I didn't ask for your advice so just hurry up and leave man; damn."

Chad went to check everything out in the dining room. It was perfect; now, if he could get rid of his annoying brother in time, the evening would be perfect. Before he could give it another thought, he got the notice from downstairs that Blaire was on her way up. She made it to the door before Nigel could leave. Chad opened the door to greet her. She was beautiful as usual. He invited her inside. Nigel walked up behind Chad. When he saw Blaire, he was disappointed. He looked at Chad and said sarcastically,

"Now I see why you were trying to get rid of me. Have a great date, Bro." He left without speaking to Blaire.

"Wow, he sure seems disappointed. What's eating him?"

"Oh nothing; don't pay him any mind."

"I've been seeing you for weeks now, and I still can't tell you two apart. I can't believe it. I mean, you guys look so much alike. You even sound alike. Can your mom tell you apart?"

"Yes, she can. With both hands clutching her purse, Chad placed his hand on the small of her back and led her to the living area. She was in awe over his home's designs and unique furnishings.

"Wow, this is amazing. It's so exquisite. Did you design this?"

"Every single inch."

Blaire was used to seeing beautiful things, but she was taken aback by what Chad could do to a home.

"Wow, not only do you design yachts, but you design condos as well. You should add interior design for homes to your repertoire. This place is gorgeous. Look at that magnificent ceiling. Oh, and the ocean view; you must have the best view in South Beach?"

"Please come, allow me to show you around."

After showing his extensive art collection and the lovely one-of-a-kind designs, she asked,

"May I see where you sleep? You can tell a lot about a man by looking at his bedroom." He took her to his bedroom. She was even more impressed.

"Wow, even the view from your bedroom is amazing. I love it. It looks as if a lady designed this." She cut her eyes towards his bed. She noticed it was a California King.

"Look at the size of that bed. I love that bed. There's enough room in there for an army. Perhaps one day I'll get to sleep in it." He took her into a side room off the corner and said,

"My wine collection features the finest wines import-ed from all over the world." She looked over his wine collection, reading each one, some she could barely pro-nounce. She was impressed.

"You have impeccable taste." They made their way back towards the living area of the condo. Blaire said, "The family chef is downstairs waiting to bring everything I'll need to prepare our dinner tonight. I wanted to come first before I had him come into your unit to set everything up. She called the chef up, and he was allowed to come in and set up the food, and he left.

She prepared pan-seared lamb chops with a rosemary balsamic reduction, garlic sautéed asparagus and roasted potatoes, a refreshing fruit salad, and a simple yet elegant chocolate mousse with a hint of rum. They enjoyed playful kisses and flirtatious talks. She allowed him to sample some of the foods as she was preparing them. He opened a bottle of the best wine from his collection, and they sipped it while waiting for dinner. After dinner, they retired to the living area. She asked permission to kick off her shoes. She did, and he rubbed her feet. He took the remote and put on some soothing romantic music. She laid her head on his shoulder, and they talked while listening to music. As the sun began to set in the Miami sky, he dimmed the lights to ensure they would enjoy the views of the city's skyline coupled with the ocean. She moved her head to his chest. The scent of his cologne brought her comfort. He could tell by her body language that she wanted to be kissed. As their lips met, he couldn't help but feel the electricity between them. As he was kissing her, his heart seemed to melt for her.

This was no ordinary woman. He wanted her. Not only in a sexual way, but he wanted all of her spirit, soul, and body. She never hid her feelings for him. She wanted him from the moment she saw him. She was willing to give him all of her, and that's exactly what she intended to do. Romantic music continued to play in the background. The effects of the wine and her undying attraction to him caused her to desire him. She longed for his strong hands to grip her body. She wanted to feel the magnitude of his passion for her. After a heated kiss, she helped him undress. She loosened his tie just enough to go over his head. She helped him with his shirt. They both fell back on the sofa, kissing passionately as before. This was it. The moment she had been waiting for was finally happening. She took his love and inserted it into her eagerly awaiting body. She slid down on him, threw her head back, and exhaled. She whispered,

"You're so huge," as she rode him with perfect rhythm. Although wet from anticipation, her body was tight around his member.

"I knew you were going to be perfect," she whispered as she continued to ride him. He took her waist and slightly pulled her down on him. Knowing he was rather large, he didn't want to harm her, so he allowed her to take the lead as he helped her with her balance. She was so excited she couldn't control her orgasms, nor could she control the screams of pleasure. She fell onto his chest.

Moved by her sexual desire for him, he held her tight. He looked at her. She slightly lifted her head and stared at him with beautiful brown eyes. She said, "I want more."

He placed her on the edge of the large sofa. He got on his knees. He leaned in, ravishing her body with his kisses, anticipating enjoying every bit of her. The delicate scent of her perfume put him in a hypnotic state. Kissing her naval, he moved down to her dripping wet sweetness. She arched her back as he kissed her clitoris. His hands caressed her curves as he indulged himself. Her flower opened, giving him the nectar he so desired.

He lost himself in loving her. This feat weakened her. She mouthed the words, *"Oh my god, please don't stop."* She caressed his shoulders as he lifted her legs to taste more of her. His tongue reached far inside, wanting to taste every bit of the honey her body could produce. "Oh my god," she screamed. He stopped and placed her on her knees on the edge of the sofa. Again, he slid his tongue into her from behind. He placed his mouth over her pussy. She was coming to a climax, for sure. He wanted to please her, and he wanted to taste more of her. His penis stiffened as she backed her body to his mouth. She gave him all he wanted.

He helped her down gently, placing her on her back with her hips on the edge of the sofa again. He inserted himself inside her. She could feel the walls of her body expand as his member began to swell. With each pulsating thrust, he loved her body until he exploded. This was only the prelude to what would be a night filled with passion. He lifted her and took her into his bedroom. They made love the rest of the night.

What neither of them noticed was that Nigel had come in and stood in the background, watching the entire scene. Nigel wanted her for himself. He knew he had to have her. Feeling his brother had cheated him, he was upset. He thought, "I should be the one with her, *not him. I can make her feel things she's never felt before.*" But how was he going to do that? His brother beat him to her.

Breakfast the following day...

Blaire spent the night at Chad's place. Chad called room service and ordered breakfast. After breakfast, they made love again. She lay on her back and whispered breathlessly,

"You're one amazing lover. You're the best." He kissed her and said,

"You're quite amazing yourself."

"It's been ages for me. It's a little tricky dating in the public eye, especially if the media catches wind of it, so I chose not to. When I met you, I knew I had to get to know you. I was attracted to you from the moment I saw you, Chad. There was just something about you. I even told my mother. I've had my eye on you for a while. I overheard a few women on my staff discussing you. They were passing around an article featuring your work in the Miami business magazine. They were discussing how handsome you were, and the article mentioned you were an eligible bachelor. When they showed me the article, I had to agree. You were very handsome and accomplished. I was happy to have met you in person. I know I came on a little strong, but I had to have you. I can remember a few times lying in my bed dreaming of being right here with you. I imagined us kissing and making love. It's funny because I can't remember having a crush on a guy like this before." She began kissing his chest. "I hope I wasn't too frisky for you," she said.

"You were perfect." They lounged around for about another hour. They showered and got dressed.

"I have a few meetings today," she said. I hope to see you soon."

"I'm looking forward to it. Allow me to walk you down to your car," he said.

He escorted her to her car with the driver. He didn't want her to leave and she didn't want to go. While standing there, he wanted to kiss her, but he waited for her to take the lead. She lightly tugged at his shirt, pulling him towards her. She stood on the tips of her toes and kissed him passionately. She didn't care who saw them. He embraced her. While they were saying their goodbyes, a couple of photographers came out of hiding and began snapping photos of them. Chad protected Blaire with his body and gently pushed her into the car's back seat. He closed her door, tapped the top of the vehicle, and the driver sped away. He went back inside trying to rid himself of his unwanted visitors.

One of them asked,

"How long have you been seeing Blaire Kensington? Is it serious between the two of you?"

He was upset at the photographer, and he hurried into the building while security escorted them from the premises. His cell phone rang. It was Blaire.

"Chad, I want to apologize to you about those photographers. They're like sharks. When they smell blood in the water, they come running."

"Actually, I was more worried about you," he told her.

"I'm used to it by now. I want you to know that this could be just the beginning. I thought they were done covering my life. I'm not sure where they came from but I'm sure they won't let up. Do you think you can handle that type of press?"

"If you can handle it then so can I." She smiled and held the phone with both hands remembering the wonderful time they shared. She said,

"I'd rather be seen with you more than any other guy." He chuckled and said, "Same here." They chatted a little more and reluctantly ended their phone call.

Nigel walked into the dining area where Chad was sitting. Sulking he said, "Now I see why you wouldn't hook me up with little miss rich girl. I guess you wanted her all to yourself."

"Nigel, I'm not responsible for fixing you up with women; besides, I disapprove of the way you treat them. Blaire was a client of mine, and given your track record with women, I didn't want to see her hurt. You tried talking to her, but she wasn't feeling you."

"That's because you hogged the conversation, and you smothered her all night."

"I never tried to step in your way. Blaire set her affections on me. I never came on to her. I didn't want to cross those boundaries, but when she made her feelings known, I couldn't help but notice my attraction to her as well. You're just going to have to face it. You can't have every woman. Blaire is looking for something more long-term. You said yourself that you're not interested in anything other than sex, and you definitely don't want to have sex with the same woman over and over again. Now tell me, what do you have to offer Blaire?"

"Evidently not much. I guess you decided to rescue her with your dick, huh?"

"Nigel, I'm not about to discuss my relationship with Blaire with you. I don't owe you an explanation. You need to focus on getting your shit together. Check in on your company, or whatever it is you do around here while I'm gone. I'm going to work."

Nigel was upset about the relationship that was taking place between the two. Every chance he got, he tried to come between them. He flirted with Blaire as often as he could. He enjoyed the fact that she couldn't tell them apart and the loving look she would give him when she thought he was Chad. He learned her daily schedule and would follow her and watch her unbeknownst to her or Chad. He would bump into her on many occasions. A few times when she'd be dining alone, he would crash her lunch as if it were a mere coincidence. He would sit and dine with her. She thought he was a little odd, but because she cared for his brother, she tried to be as friendly as possible. He read more into her kindness and the warm smiles she would give him. The more he saw her, the more obsessed he became.

His days were filled with thoughts of her. He would watch as his brother made love to her wishing it was him instead. When she spent the night at Chad's place, he would leave her asleep in his bedroom while he went to work. Nigel would watch her as she slept and pleasure himself. He also watched as she showered. Nigel was becoming delusional daily, and, in his mind, he had begun to develop a love affair and fantasies of her, which he intended to fulfill no matter the cost.

Confident of his ability to persuade women as he had done many times before, he reasoned in his mind if he could get her alone for a while, he would cause her to fall in love with him and forget all about his brother. At least, that was his plan. He just needed to be patient and wait for the right moment.

THE PROPOSAL

Chad and Blaire were going strong a year later. It was official; they were a couple. Chad was finally happy. The love he had for Blaire was unlike any he'd experienced before. He was willing to put in the time necessary to be with her. She spent a lot of time at his place, and he spent time at hers. Once the relationship had become serious, Blaire wanted her family to get to know him. They made dinner plans with her parents. It was time for Chad to formally meet her parents as her mate. Chad picked her up from her place, and they rode together to her parents' home. She noticed he was looking a bit nervous. She took his hand and held it with a reassuring grip.

"Are you okay?" she asked. He looked at her with a cool, calm expression and said,

"Of course, I'm okay; why wouldn't I be? I'm only meeting your father who has a reputation for being a shrewd man."

"Oh, you'll be fine. You've met him many times before so why are you so nervous?"

"I met him when we were only friends. He didn't know about us. Now that he'll know that we're a couple, he may not approve."

"Why wouldn't he approve?"

"He may not think I'm good enough for you. Perhaps he has an ideal person in mind for you. He's a billionaire, for goodness sake; you're practically royalty."

"Chad babe, you're a great guy, and I love you. Dad will see that, too. All he wants is for me to be happy; besides, Mother adores you." They pulled up to the estate and went inside. Chad had a bottle of wine and flowers to present to her parents, who were waiting for them.

Chad was a gentleman who went to Mrs. Kensington first and said hello. He handed her the bouquet. He went to Blaire's father next, and they shook hands. He passed him the bottle of wine. Mr. Kensington set the wine on the coffee table. He was a large, heavy-set giant of a man. He was wearing a short-sleeved linen shirt with matching slacks. His belly stood out, and one could tell he was a man given to appetite. He looked every bit of the southern Caucasian guy. Blaire's parents seemed like an unlikely couple. Delighted to see his daughter, he greeted her with a warm hug and a kiss. He was a doting father. Blaire, still holding her father's hand, began to speak.

"Mom, Dad, as you may know, Chad and I have been friends for almost a year now, and we've become very close in these last few months. We've grown quite fond of each other."

She released her father's hand, walked over, and stood by Chad.

"We're officially announcing to you that we're a couple. We care for each other very much, and I love him." She looked at Chad. He smiled and squeezed her hand.

"He's a great guy. Now, Dad, I know you didn't approve of my last boyfriend, and rightly so, but Chad is so different from him, and he's good to me."

Mr. Kensington, eyeing his daughter, not saying anything good or bad, reached into his humidor and got a cigar. He reached for his favorite pair of guillotine cigar cutters and clipped the edge of the large cigar while his gaze fell upon Chad. He tilted his head and gave Chad an unapproving look. Chad swallowed the lump in his throat. After clipping the end and lighting it, he let out a few puffs of smoke and said to his daughter with an extreme southern drawl,

"So, you think you like this one, huh?"

"Yes, Daddy, I like him a lot."

He continued looking Chad over. He was smiling nervously, but he was looking at Blaire with an adoring look. Mr. Kensington could tell that Chad's feelings were mutual by his demeanor. He decided to toy with him a little to make him sweat, asking him the most difficult and uncomfortable questions a father could ask a man dating his daughter. Chad answered all questions most honestly and sincerely. Afterwards, he said,

"Chad son, let me holler at you for a minute." Chad stood to his feet, kissed Blaire, and excused himself. Mr. Kensington grabbed the bottle of wine Chad gave him and led him to the bar in an adjacent room just out of ear-shot of the ladies. Blaire was excited, and she beamed with pride, telling her mother about Chad as she had done many times before. Mr. Kensington motioned for Chad to have a seat. He told his employee to fix him a drink. He offered Chad a drink, but he quickly declined. He asked for privacy after his drink was handed to him.

As they were waiting for the employee to leave the room, he looked at Chad with a slight frown as to intimidate his opponent as a boxer would do to his rival before a match. He didn't say much further causing Chad to wonder what he could be thinking. Finally, he said,

"Relax young man, don't look so stiff." Chad let out a nervous sigh.

"2000 Chateau Lafite Rothschild Bordeaux. Not bad, son," he said, looking at the bottle of wine Chad had brought for dinner. "Do you know a lot about wines?" he asked.

"I'm a collector," Chad said. "If you place that one on hold for another ten years or so, it will age nicely, or you can enjoy it today if you wish. I purchased it a few years ago. I do hope that you'll enjoy it."

"I'm sure I will."

They began to talk. The more they talked, the more Blaire's father liked what he heard and saw in him. He screened him for any signs of deception and weakness. Blaire wasn't aware that her father knew she and Chad had been dating. He had him checked out, and he was impressed; more than that, he was impressed that he was a self-made man. He loved the fact that he was a man of principle and a disciplined guy who not only helped and supported his family but also gave back to the community. He had no problem with his daughter seeing him. Chad assured him that his intentions were not to harm his daughter but to love her and ensure her happiness. After spending more time with Mr. Kensington, he was convinced that he cared for Blaire, and he felt he had her best interest at heart, so he approved of their relationship.

A couple of months had passed since Chad officially met Blaire's parents. They often shared luncheons and dinners with them. Chad and Mr. Kensington were becoming close, and he even offered him a chance at business opportunities within his circle of acquaintances. Chad's schedule was even busier, and he hired another assistant for his Miami location. He planned on expanding his business as well as that of his brother's back in Little Rock. Nigel stayed over in Miami while Chad was looking forward to taking Blaire to Arkansas to spend some much-needed time with her there.

After being in Arkansas for a couple of days, Blaire realized the natives lived at a slower, mellow pace than Miami. She enjoyed the lush greenery, the beautiful land,

and all the charm of the Natural state. She enjoyed boating, camping, and fishing, all in a luxurious atmosphere. She couldn't believe the calm and peace and the many serene cubby holes the state had to offer. Even the restaurants were great. The dining experiences and the southern cuisine made her love it even more. It was quite a change from Miami. Chad's mother invited the couple to a family and friends dinner party. His parents lived twenty minutes outside the city limits of Little Rock on a ten-acre spread with a private lake. They moved there when Chad and Nigel were in their early teens in a much smaller house. Chad demolished the old house and built their present home with all the amenities they desired to make the home more enjoyable. His father owned a couple of boats, which they kept out back. Chad had a deck built out into the water so that his mother could go fishing any time she wanted without her having to get in the boat with his father.

Blaire was excited to meet her beau's parents, especially his mother. Mrs. Lancaster greeted them at the door. She smiled as she saw how beautiful Blaire was. Blaire handed her a gift bag and hugged her. Mrs. Lancaster wore a peach skirt suit which showed her shapely legs. Legs that would deceive the onlooker into thinking she was much younger than she was. She worked out daily with her good friend Annette Barnes. Her hair was shoulder length and curled with one side pinned up, revealing her youthful, light-toned face.

Blaire said, "You look lovely. I hope I look this good when I'm in my early forties."

Chad's mother said, "Oh look at you, I like you already. We're going to get along just fine."

Mr. Lancaster stood at his feet, ready to greet her. He was around five feet nine inches tall and of medium build. He and Chad looked similar except for the salt-and-pepper mustache and hair. He had brown-toned skin. He wore grey dress slacks, a nice, collared shirt, and a necktie. She complimented him as well.

"You and Chad could pass for brothers," she said. They went into the living area of the home and talked until the rest of the guests began arriving. She met his grandparents, aunts and uncles, cousins, and close family friends. They enjoyed themselves. The event had a family reunion feel. Good southern cooking and great laughs. After dinner, they sat around and told embarrassing childhood stories about Chad and Nigel and his cousins. Blaire enjoyed hearing all about his shenanigans as a kid. When they brought out the pictures and videos, the fun really began. Blaire was accepted into his family. Money wasn't a factor neither was fame. All of them were one, from the person who had hundreds in the bank to the ones who had millions. They were family and they enjoyed each other's company.

After hanging out much of the day, it was starting to get late. Neither of them wanted the evening to end.

Chad and the family said their goodbyes and he and Blaire left.

"You have an amazing family. Your parents are wonderful people. I enjoyed them so much. I could've stayed for hours." He smiled at her and lifted her hand to kiss it.

"They enjoyed you too, especially mom."

"I love it here in Arkansas; everyone is so friendly. It's beautiful here. It's much quieter, and not one single reporter has bothered us since we've been here. I love Miami, but I'm starting to like it here, too. I had never given much thought to the state. The most I know about it is a former president was born here. Now that I'm seeing it for myself, I think it's a nice place. I think father needs to begin thinking about buying property here."

"You haven't seen anything yet; you still have to check out our national parks, lakes, and streams during the fall season. The autumn colors are magnificent"

"I'm looking forward to it."

They went to Chad's home, where they spent the evening together making love. They both slept in that entire day. Chad conducted a couple of video conferences in his office and chose to spend the day with his love. He needed the time off. He had been such a workaholic that he made no time for his personal life. He intended to change that. Blaire was the greatest thing that happened to him, and he wanted to express his love for her by making her his wife.

He secretly spoke with her parents and told them of his intent to propose. After a long discussion with her father and speaking with her mother, they both gave him their blessing. Her father made it clear that although he approved, he wanted his daughter, and their family finances protected. Chad knew what that meant, and he agreed. He invited both of their parents to witness the proposal. When the day came, he was full of nervous excitement. He'd never done anything like this, but he's never loved anyone like he loved Blaire. He made reservations at one of Little Rock's exclusive restaurants. He wouldn't have it any other way. He reserved a special table and forwarded his plans to management. He sent a car for her parents and another to his parent's home.

Blaire had no clue what he was up to, and she didn't know her parents were meeting them for dinner. She was happy to be spending time with Chad. Once at the restaurant they were seated.

"Why such a large table?" She asked.

"It was the only one they had left. I tried to pull some strings to get us a smaller table, but this was all I could get on such short notice. I hope you're not disappointed."

"As long as I'm with you, I don't care where we're seated," she said. Not long after they were seated, his parents came in, and he pretended as if they were there by chance.

"Babe look, there are my parents. Hey, do you mind if they sit with us tonight baby?"

"Of course, they can, you know I don't mind," she said. He invited them to sit with them. Still clueless Blaire said,

"Well, that worked out just fine because we have enough room at our table." She greeted his parents with joy. A few minutes later, her parents walked in. When she noticed her parents coming into the restaurant, she knew something was up. She lightly hit Chad on the arm and smiled at him. She ran into her father's arms. She turned to her mother for a quick hug, and they walked over to their table. Chad seated her mother then he seated Blaire. He shook her father's hand and took his seat.

"What are you doing here guys?" She asked.

"We just came by to see what you two kids were up to." She looked at Chad and said,

"You planned this all along, didn't you?" He shrugged his shoulders and smiled.

"I don't know what you are talking about sweetheart." She kissed him.

"Un-huh... I'm sure you don't." Chad introduced their parents. They made small talk.

Blaire's father asked, "Chad son, what does a man have to do to get a good stiff drink around here?"

"Let's see what we can make happen Mr. Kensington." Chad motioned for the staff to attend to their needs. At the end of dinner, Chad slightly pushed his seat back. He stood up and said,

"Mom, Dad, Mr. and Mrs. Kensington, I brought you here this evening because I want you to share in the love that Blaire and I share." Chad continued speaking, looking at her father.

"Mr. Kensington, I love your daughter, and I plan on taking great care of her and spending the rest of my life making her the happiest woman on this earth." He turned his attention towards Blaire. "Blaire ever since I met you, you've taught me how to live again. You've shown me how to let go and laugh, to take chances, to take leaps of faith. You taught me what it truly means to love someone with my whole heart. I'm honored to be your man. Would do me the honor of becoming my wife?" He reached in his pocket and pulled out the ring and asked,

"Ms. Blaire Kensington, will you marry me?"

With her mouth hanging open and her hand on her chest, she was delighted. She looked toward her parents. They were smiling and her father looked on in approval. Her mother nodded her head. She looked at his parents who were also smiling and before she knew anything she was screaming,

"Oh my god yes!" Chad placed the ring on her finger. She had tears in her eyes, and she was trembling with excitement. He held her until she stopped shaking. As soft music played in the background on his queue, he took her to an open space in the restaurant, and they danced. Their parents and a few other couples also joined them. The air was filled with romance for all who witnessed their love. Even their parents were in a romantic mood.

Mr. Kensington said, "Chad, my son, you have started something. I'm going to take my wife back to our suite and spend some quality time with her." Blaire's mother smiled and hugged her husband.

"It has been a while you old romantic devil you."

Chad's father said, "Congratulations." His mother hugged Blaire and said, "Congratulations sweetie."

"I love you, son; congratulations."

"Thanks Mom. I love you. Thanks for coming. It meant so much to me." Both their parents left.

"Do you want dessert?"

"Are you kidding who can eat dessert after all of this?" She looked at her ring. "How about having me for dessert?"

"Oh, you know I have a sweet tooth, don't you? I can't wait to get you home. I have an insatiable appetite for you."

While Chad and Blaire were celebrating their love in Arkansas, Nigel was still in Miami. He had finally gotten a place of his own. He spent his days thinking of Blaire. He allowed thoughts of her making love to his brother to play in his head. He resented Chad for having her. He saved photos on his computer that he had taken of her without her knowledge. The more images he saw of her, the more he wanted her. His desire for her went far beyond obsession. It was downright maddening. With each woman he bedded he would imagine she was Blaire.

While hanging out at a Latin nightclub he met a couple of women, one a twenty-one-year-old named Sophia, the other a twenty-three-year-old named Adriana. After several drinks, he took them to his place for sex. After sleeping with them both they all fell asleep. He was awakened by the women playfully sexing each other while playing with his half-erect penis. He opened his eyes to see it was Sofia who had him in her hand. She leaned in and put her warm mouth on his shaft. She smiled as it began to swell in her mouth. Adriana joined her; both girls were taking turns sucking him. Just when he was about to cum, Sofia climbed atop him. Nigel looked over at the television which had been left on. On the screen was a tabloid show in which Chad and Blaire were being featured. He reached for the remote turning the TV off. He was no longer interested in his companion, who was giving it her all, trying to please him and herself in the process. He pushed her off.

"What's wrong?" She asked.

"Nothing, get dressed, the both of you." He got out of bed, gave them both money, and quickly escorted them to the door. After getting his laptop, he went through his pictures of Blaire. His phone rang. It was his mother calling about his brother's engagement. She was excited for her son, and she had been telling everyone who would listen about the engagement and to whom he was getting married. Nigel answered the phone.

"Hi, Nigel."

"Hi mom, how are you doing?"

"I'm doing okay. I have some news about your brother"

"What is it, mom?"

"He and Blaire are getting married. Isn't that great?" He was speechless.

"Son, did you hear me? I said your brother is getting married." Sickened by the news he snapped at her.

"I heard you Mom." She could hear the negative tone in his voice.

"Well, aren't you happy for him?"

"Yes, okay, Mom. I have to go. Let me call you right back, okay?"

He was upset. He looked at Blaire's picture, and he got angrier. In a fit of rage, he flung his laptop across the room. Over the next few days, the news magazines and tabloids reported on the engagement, which further fueled his jealousy. He always got what he wanted, and he wanted Blaire. He was determined not to let anyone get in his way, not even his brother. He had to stop this wedding, but how? He began to plot his next move.

CHAPTER THREE

Work on the Kensington yacht was wrapping up, so Chad planned a trip to Miami to check on its progress. This job was a personal one for him, as it belonged to his future father-in-law, and he wanted it to outshine any vessel he'd ever designed before. The plan was to have it ready by his birthday, but they went a little over with the designs, so it took a little longer than expected.

Chad and Blaire were searching for a beautiful lake-front property in Arkansas so they could build a home once they were married, a personal space of their very own. The thought of living in her fiancé's native state appealed to her. She would keep her properties in Miami. As with Chad, they would commute to Miami from Arkansas as needed. Two of Blaire's favorite longtime staff members offered to make the move to Arkansas to assist her as needed. She'd given them a few weeks to gather their belongings before joining her. Chad walked into the den where she was lounging on the sofa.

"Hello Mrs. Lancaster," he said, kissing her on the cheek. She smiled and repeated what he said.

"Mrs. Lancaster; that sounds so lovely. I can hardly wait."

"So, my beautiful wife-to-be, what are you going to do while I'm away?"

"Hmm, let's see. I'll be looking for property and planning our wedding. Oh, and I'm going to brunch with your mother tomorrow. I think it's a good idea for us to spend more time together. She's such a sweet lady; and who knows, I may even get lucky and get a little inside information on my future husband. I want to be a great wife for you."

"You're already fabulous," he said, stealing another kiss. He began to gather more of his things for his trip to Florida. Blaire walked over to him and straightened his tie. Kissing him on the lips, she said,

"Hurry home, babe. I'll see you next week."

"I wish you would come with me, Blaire."

"Perhaps I'll fly over in the next few days, but we'll see. I told you; I really would like to spend some time with your mother. You don't want me to start on a bad foot with my mother-in-law, do you?"

Taking her by the hand and lifting it to his lips, he kissed the back of it.

"I guess not. You two ladies behave while I'm gone."

"What kind of trouble can I get into hanging out with your mother?"

"You'd be surprised." He chuckled. They share a passionate kiss.

"It's so hard leaving you." She walked him to the door and watched as he got into the car and drove away. She went back to bed. She took Chad's pillow and held it close to her body. His scent was still there. She slept for a few hours. After her nap, she got a little work done, and then she called her mother. They discussed her wedding plans for the better part of an hour. She lounged around for the rest of the evening looking at properties in the area. She also browsed the internet for wedding ideas until she got sleepy. She ordered dinner, had it delivered, and then she went to sleep. The following morning, she began her day with a phone call to Chad. She showered and got dressed. Afterwards, she called Chad's mother.

"Hello Mrs. Lancaster."

"Hello dear."

"I'll be on my way just as soon as the driver gets here."

"You don't have to send for the driver. I'll drive us today."

"Thank you, but we're going to need a driver. I want to enjoy your company. I planned a full day. We're going shopping, dining, and whatever else we choose. I just need you to point me to the best places to dine and shop. Neither of us needs the stress of driving."

Mrs. Lancaster agreed, and they ended their call. When her car pulled up to the family home, she went inside. Mrs. Lancaster greeted her. They proceeded to the family room, where a very beautiful elderly woman was sitting. She, too, was extremely toned and wore clothing that showed off her beautiful body. The grey strands of hair told her that she was a little older, but she was a great-looking woman. Mrs. Lancaster introduced them.

"Blaire this is Annette Barnes. We've been friends for over forty years, she's practically family. Annette, meet Chad's finance, Blaire Kensington."

"It's nice to meet you, Mrs. Barnes. You're lovely," she said, shaking her hand. "So, you ladies have been friends for over forty years? You know I read an article somewhere that says if you've been friends longer than ten years, you're officially cousins." They laughed. Mrs. Annette Barnes said,

"Girl, Chad did well, didn't he? And to think, you were worried he may not find a good enough girl to marry. She's beautiful, and she has her own money. From what I hear, you're a very nice girl. When are you two going to have babies, sweetheart, because Lord knows Delores here has been longing for grandbabies for years?"

"Chad and I are hoping to make an announcement very soon," she replied.

"So, does that mean you're already preg….? Blaire interrupted her. She placed her index finger to her lips, pursed them, and said,

"Shh." Mrs. Barnes winked and nodded her head. They talked for about thirty minutes. "Mrs. Barnes, why don't you join us today? It will be a lady's day out and we can all get to know each other better."

"That's a wonderful idea, Blaire," said Mrs. Lancaster. The ladies went out on the town and enjoyed themselves. Afterward, they went back to Chad's parents' home, where they conversed. Mrs. Lancaster brought out a tray of fresh fruit, cheeses, and a bottle of wine. She poured Blaire a glass.

"I'm so sorry, Mrs. Lancaster. May I have water instead?"

"Sure."

She placed the glass in front of Mrs. Barnes instead and got water for Blaire.

"Mrs. Lancaster, when I came over the other day, I noticed the smell of fresh desserts. What were you baking?"

"I was baking butter-crusted peach cobbler and a fresh apple cake. These men around here would sell their souls for those desserts."

"You do make the best peach cobbler this side of the state girl," replied Mrs. Barnes.

"Mrs. Lancaster, I would love to make something special for Chad when he comes home. He enjoys a nice home-cooked meal. I would love to be able to make a dish he's familiar with. We have several chefs and I'm skilled in the kitchen making Mexican dishes handed down by my mother and grandmother, but you just can't beat a southern-cooked meal, especially when your love prefers it. I think a personal touch by me occasionally would be awesome. Do you think you could share the recipe with me?"

"I suppose I could since you *are* going to be his wife. But if I share it with you, please don't give the recipe to anyone else. It's been in my family for many years."

"I promise I won't Mrs. Lancaster. You have my word."

After spending the day with Chad's mother, Blaire returned to Chad's place. While on her way, Chad called. She smiled when she heard his voice.

"Hello darling, how did your day go?"

"Oh, Chad, it was beautiful. I spent the day with your mother and her friend Mrs. Barnes. They are such lovely ladies. We had a fabulous day."

"I know my mother talked your ears off, didn't she?"

"I love her; she's a great lady. We enjoyed our time together. They're two of the most spirited ladies I've met in quite a while."

"I'm glad they kept you busy while I'm here. I must stay over in Miami for a few more days. You can fly over if you'd like."

"I miss you, but I think I'll stay here in Arkansas and wait for you. I sent for two of my employees to assist me around here while we're here. They'll be flying over in about a week. Besides, I love it here. It's so peaceful. Oh, and I have a surprise for you when you arrive."

"A surprise? What kind of surprise? Can you give me a hint?"

"No, you'll just have to wait and see."

They talked until she reached his place. She released her driver for the night and went inside. After ending her call with Chad, she showered, called her parents, and went to sleep. Chad called Nigel to remind him to check on his company after the liaison he hired reported some things that needed both Chad's and Nigel's attention. He hadn't heard from Nigel in a couple of days. After getting no answer, he worked a little longer and fell asleep in his office.

Blaire was awakened by a kiss on her cheek. She opened her eyes and noticed Chad standing over her. She was pleasantly surprised to see him. She immediately wrapped her arms around his neck and kissed him.

"I thought you weren't coming home for a few days." She helped him with his shirt as they passionately kissed.

"I missed you so much!" He kissed her neck and leaned his body into hers. As he hovered over her, still kissing her, she opened his pants. He ripped her panties off and began to love her with his mouth.

"Mmm, yes, baby, I missed you, and I missed this." He feverishly sucked and kissed her wetness as she moaned, moving her hips to the rhythm of his tongue. Her pleasure level was heightened to peaks that propelled her into a cosmic world.

"Umm baby, I'm so glad to be marrying you. I can have this for the rest of my life."

The more he loved her with his mouth, the more excited she became until she could no longer hold back.

"That's it, baby. Give it to me."

As she thought of taking him in, she began to salivate. He teased her by not giving in to her, making her want him even more. He relented and laid back and let her have her way. She was excited to see how big his member had swollen. She had never seen it quite so erect. She tried to put it in her mouth but was having a little difficulty tackling the monstrosity of a muscle.

"Wow, Chad, you missed me too, I see. I've never seen you this excited." She did her best at working on what she wanted. She could tell by the movement of his body that he was about to explode in her mouth. He held her hair as she continued to share the warmth of her mouth. His eyes rolled back in his head, but he wanted to watch her perform. She looked glorious to him. His heart ached within. She was turning him out, and he couldn't hold it any longer. He began to moan. She continued until suddenly; he gently pushed her head back and flipped her onto the bed. She wrapped her legs around his neck and locked her ankles together. He pumped her until he released his load into her. They both climaxed together and ended up intertwined in a massive heap of sweaty bodies.

He rarely said a word. He continued making love to her the rest of the night and well into the morning. She was exhausted. She wanted to please him, so she continued to give herself to him for as long as he needed.

"Damn baby, did you take some Viagra or something? You've never made love to me like this before," she said.

He said nothing but continued sexing her until he was tired and his dick was sensitive to the touch. He then motioned for her to suck him off one more time. She obliged as he came once more. He had nothing left in him. He had given her everything. He nodded off. She was relieved. She went into the kitchen to make a pot of coffee. She heard her phone ringing. She didn't want to wake Chad, so she answered quickly. It was Chad's phone calling her! *Why would his phone be calling me when he's lying in the bed asleep?* she thought. She ignored it, got her coffee, and got back in bed. She got the remote and flipped on the TV. Streams of sunlight peered through the drapes and brightened the room; she noticed a small growth on his side which looked like a mole. She moved in closer to investigate.

"I don't remember seeing that before."

Her phone rang again, startling her. This time, she answered without looking at the caller ID. The voice on the other end sounded cheerful.

"Good morning, baby! How are you this morning?"

She was confused. The voice on the other end sounded like Chad, but he was lying in bed next to her.

"Who is this?" she asked.

"It's me, baby, your fiancé," he said jokingly, knowing that she would catch on.

"Chad?"

She looked at the man lying in bed and quickly tried to get out. Hearing her concern, he sprinted towards Blaire and took the phone from her.

"I can explain," he said.

He grabbed her phone and ended the call and tried to pretend he was Chad for a minute. She began to replay the events of the previous night. Putting everything together, she realized that she'd been tricked.

"Nigel?" She screamed.

"Okay, I know you're angry but let me explain. Blaire, I love you. I wanted you from the moment I laid eyes on you. You wouldn't have anything to do with me. Since we met, I've done nothing but think of you. I can't get you out of my head. I've never been taken with any woman as I am with you. I want you, Blaire. I'm the one who deserves to be with you, not my brother. You know it's true. Why you said yourself while we were making love that no one had ever made you feel the way I made you feel."

"That's because I thought you were Chad! How could you do something like this to me? How could you do this to your brother?"

"Don't you understand? I had no other choice. How else was I going to get you to notice me? If you really loved him so much, why didn't you notice the difference in our lovemaking? I made your body feel something it's never felt before. The way you responded to me and to my touch your body literally exploded with excitement. Admit it." She was angered by what she was hearing. She knew there was no reasoning with him by the look in his eyes. He was psychotic. She feared for her safety.

"Nigel, I love your brother. We're going to be married. I would never have knowingly slept with you." He held both her arms and tried to kiss her. She turned her head.

"But you loved it, didn't you? You loved every minute of it. The way you rode my dick, the way you sucked me off, the way you took me in, and you; you tasted so sweet. Please let me taste you again."

He tried to push her back on the bed. She struggled a little. Realizing that he was much stronger than she was and not knowing what he was capable of, she played it cool. He laid her on the bed and pulled her nightgown up. He began to kiss her body. She cringed. She held her breath hoping he would stop. The more he engaged himself, the angrier she became. Her body was tense. He thought that she was enjoying him, but she was busy planning her escape. She continued to try to talk him out of what he was doing but to no avail.

She felt her body was betraying her by naturally responding, producing an unwanted orgasm. She was angry with herself for allowing it to happen. He could tell, and it gave him the false impression that she was enjoying it.

"See I knew you loved it." Afterwards, he climbed atop her and inserted himself into her. Again, her body responded even though her mind didn't. Nigel was so preoccupied with his assault on her that he hadn't realized that she had reached for the lamp on the nightstand. She hit him over the head with it. Jumping out of the bed, she ran for the bedroom door. Her feet were tangled in the covers, and she tripped, falling face down on the floor. Nigel caught her and pulled her back to the bed.

"Blaire, why are you running? Can't you see I want you?"

"But I don't want you. Why can't you understand that?"

"You will. I know you can't love my brother. Look at how you keep making love to me."

"Is that what you think? You raped me. I hate you. I don't want you. You make my skin crawl."

"No, I turned you on sexually admit it. You think I didn't notice how you responded to me?"

"My body may have responded, but my mind wasn't in it." Realizing that he was becoming more unstable, she tried bargaining with him.

"Look, Nigel. Let me go, and I won't mention this to anybody."

"But I want you to mention it," he said. "Tell my brother how you made love to me. Tell him how you enjoyed yourself. Tell him how you couldn't keep your hands off me. I want him to know that."

"Nigel, you're sick, and you need help." He was completely unhinged and had lost all sense of reality. He tried to force himself on her again. This time she violently fought him. He noticed a tear had fallen down her cheek.

"You disgust me you fucking maggot!" She spat in his face. Undaunted by her attempts to get him to stop, he placed the back of his forearm against her throat and applied a little pressure. "Stop fighting, Blaire." He was holding her down by force. He didn't realize she was choking. Finally, she stopped fighting. He slumped over on top of her. He was exhausted from wrestling with her. He kissed her lips.

"I love you. We're going to be together. You're going to tell Chad it's over between the two of you. You're going to be with me."

After lying there for a few seconds, he noticed that she wasn't moving. He looked down at her and noticed that her lips were blueish purple, and her eyes were rolled back in her head. He was horrified, He tried to wake her, but she didn't respond. He lightly slapped her face. He tried to resuscitate her, but his attempt to save her life was futile. He was afraid. He cleaned up the scene as best he could. He ripped the sheets from the bed and placed them in a trash bag. He took her cell phone, wiped his fingerprints from it, got his things along with the sheets, and left. He had parked his vehicle a block away when he arrived the night before. He ran to his vehicle and started driving. Distraught, he began crying uncontrollably.

"What have I done?" he asked himself repeatedly. *"Blaire, I love you; I'm so sorry, baby. I love you,"* he said screaming and crying.

In the meantime, Chad continued to call her phone. After getting no answer, he called his home phone, but still no answer. He took the first flight to Arkansas. It was going on four o'clock when his plane landed. He continued calling her until he made it to his home. Concerned for her well-being, he ran inside, leaving his keys in the entry door. He went through the house calling her name. Suddenly, he happened upon her lifeless body which was sprawled across the bed. Time stood still. He knew she was gone. His eyes scanned the room taking a mental note of everything from the missing linen to the lamp she used to hit her attacker. Her cell phone was on the nightstand. He'd hoped it was a bad dream, and he would wake at any moment, but reality was slowly sinking in. He touched her body and noticed she was already stiffening. The dead look in her eyes was as one frozen in time with pain and struggle on her face to be etched in his memory forever. He fell to the floor and cried.

He called the authorities. Next, he called her parents. It was one of the most difficult phone calls he ever had to make. After hearing the news of her death, her mother fainted. She was comforted by her equally distraught husband. They immediately flew to Arkansas. Her father wouldn't believe it until he saw her body. He had a small glimmer of hope, but he knew in his heart that Chad was telling the truth. The media began to form quickly outside the gates of Chad's home. He was still there with her when the authorities came. He sat close to her body sobbing. The paramedics motioned for him to move. After checking her vitals and confirming her death, the coroner arrived on the scene to determine the time of death while the detectives began their investigation. Nigel slipped out of town, heading back to Miami, trying to give himself an alibi. He'd finally made it to Atlanta, and he was exhausted. He was physically and emotionally drained. He was tempted to ditch his rental and catch a flight, but he knew in doing so, he would leave a paper trail, so he rested for about an hour and headed on towards Miami Beach. He disposed of the bed linen at the state line. News quickly spread of Blaire Kensington's death. News outlets and tabloids across America were reporting on the crime. By the time her parents made it into town, her body had already been taken to the county's morgue. Chad went to the airport to meet the Kensingtons. His parents were with him. As Mr. Kensington got off the plane, he saw the tears and the distressed look on Chad's face, and he immediately broke down. He knew his daughter was gone. Weighted with grief, he had to be physically escorted to the waiting vehicle. Chad placed his arm around him as they walked to the car together. His mother comforted Mrs. Kensington who could barely walk herself. While in the car, Chad continued to apologize to her father.

"I should've been there to protect her. If only she had come to Miami with me, she'd still be here. I promised you that I was going to take care of her, but I didn't. I'm so sorry Mr. Kensington. I'm going to find out who did this and I'm going to kill him myself."

They made it to the police station. The family was briefed on the outcome of the immediate investigation. They were informed of the cause of death. Chad's mother listened in horror. She could see the anger on Chad's face as he heard the news of how she died. The news was difficult for Mr. Kensington, but he needed to hear the truth.

"I need to see my baby," he demanded. He was escorted back into the exam room. When he saw his daughter's lifeless body lying on the cold, steel table, he tried to reach for her by touching her shoulder.

"Wake up, baby. It's daddy. Come on, wake for me, sweetheart."

The detective said, "Sir, I'm sorry, but we can't allow you to touch her. We don't want to compromise the integrity of the investigation, and her body hasn't been fully processed." He tried to be strong. Chad lost control of his emotions seeing the pain Mr. Kensington was experiencing.

"How soon can I take my daughter home?" he asked the detective.

"After we're done with our investigation, which should take at least another day or two, then her body will be released to the family." Mr. Kensington's heart sank. He quickly left the room. Chad followed him.

"Mr. Kensington," he called out to him while trying to catch up to him. "Mr. Kensington!" He finally caught him.

"Where are you headed, sir?"

"I have to see about my wife." Mr. Kensington took his wife by the hand and escorted her to the area where their daughter was. She said her goodbyes, and afterward, she broke down. Her husband comforted her. Once she realized the inevitable, she immediately went into mother mode, and they began making plans to take her back to Miami.

The media coverage was nationwide. The mystery of who could have killed her played out in the media. Everyone who was anyone was covering the story and doing coverage of her younger life. After holding her body for two days, she was released from the crime lab to the family. The investigation into her death continued.

A memorial service was held in her honor in Miami. Nigel attended but stayed in the background. Nobody suspected him of the murder. He didn't interact much with the family. He did his best to act as a form of emotional support for his brother, but he wasn't doing a good job of it. He took her death hard, and he grieved just as much as Chad and her parents. Chad never suspected a thing.

No one thought it odd the emotions Nigel expressed at the service. They thought he was simply being supportive of his brother. After seeing him moping around, Chad went to him and said,

"Hey, thanks man, for being here for me. I know you were fond of Blaire, and she was fond of you." He hung his head in shame. Nigel looked at him and nodded his head.

"I'm sorry man," he said.

Chad was at a loss for words. He didn't know what to say. He'd never seen his brother quite so emotional, but he was moved by his show of compassion. Nigel stayed with the family for a moment but as soon as the opportunity presented itself, he left.

Wanting to find the killer on his own, Chad flew into Little Rock hoping to find out more information about Blaire's death. He called his mother's close friend Annette Barnes. Her daughter owned a detective agency. He made an appointment to see her.

It was a long, hot day at the Barnes Detective Agency in Little Rock, Arkansas. Private investigator Jessica Barnes had previously solved a case involving a serial killer. She received lots of news coverage. She saw an uptick in her cases. After a while, things began to slow down. Recently, her latest cases consisted of mostly wealthy spouses spying on each other and processing services. She was looking for that perfect case. A big meaty one, a case she could sink her teeth into. She longed for the days when she was on the police force solving various crimes even working in the homicide division for a few years. She was a great detective. She quit the force because of conflict issues. She felt her time would be better served helping the community in her own way. She could work at her discretion without anyone looking over her shoulder. Although her family was considered wealthy, Jessica opted out of the traditional family life and chose to go into the field of law enforcement. When her parents divorced, her father left her a tiny fortune. She used part of the funds to open her private investigative firm. Her mother, Annette Barnes, is a retired paralegal. At sixty-plus years old, she spends her days working out and teaching a fitness class for seniors. When she's not doing that, she helps her daughter at the agency. In the beginning, she only helped with the secretarial duties, but as time went on, she began to take on a more active role in the agency, even becoming active in the investigations by going undercover when needed. She's also brave, not afraid of anything or anyone, and she knows her way around a weapon or two, including heavy artillery. It's no wonder her daughter is fearless. She inherited that trait from her mother.

Chad walked in the door and saw Jessica's mother sitting at her desk. She stopped typing on the computer and stood to her feet to greet him. He was like a nephew to her. "Hello Chad. I see you made it back to town. It's good to see you," she said, looking up at him with her light brown eyes and a warm smile.

"I wish I could say it's good to be home, but we both know I'd be lying. I feel so empty inside.

She gently placed her hands in his and lightly kissed him on the cheek. Jessica could hear his voice from her office, so she walked out front to meet him. She saw the look of despair on his face. She, too, greeted him warmly.

"Hi Chad, how are you holding up my friend?"

"Not well at all, Jessie." He began to sob. Jessica and her mother held him.

After an emotional moment, Jessica went to get him bottled water while her mother comforted him. Jessica entered the room again with the water and handed it to him, and he pulled himself together. He said,

"I want to thank you for coming to the memorial service for my fiancée. Your support meant more than you know."

Jessica said, "We're family here. You don't have to thank us. We love you." He smiled through tears and said,

"I apologize for being so emotional. It's just that I miss Blaire so much. We were happy together, but somebody stole it. They stole her beautiful life. I need her. They don't know the hole they've left in my heart. She was a beautiful person. Who could do such a thing to my love?" He went on for a few more minutes. He began to beat himself up.

"Calm down Chad. You're not to blame. You had no way of knowing."

"Jessie, I need you to help me find the person who did this." In short, Chad wanted Jessica to find the killer before the police could in hopes of getting revenge.

"But the police are already on the case. There's not much I can do. I would just be in their way. I think they're capable of handling this investigation," she said, motioning for him to have a seat. She got a chair and placed it directly in front of him.

"I want you to handle it for me on this end. You've solved cases that have stumped the professionals. I know you can find her killer. When you find the bastard, I'm going to kill him myself. A monster like that doesn't deserve to live, and he doesn't need a fair trial. Jessica touched him on the shoulder to calm his anger. He looked up at her. He knew she was sure to try and convince him not to seek revenge. Her long dark hair fell forward over her deep, warm brown shoulders as she moved in closer to him. He looked into her weary brown eyes. He could tell she was hurting for him. As much as he didn't want to worry her, he was on a mission and desperately needed her help.

"I know you don't mean that. You're just angry right now," she said.

"You're damn right I'm angry. I'm angry at her killer, I'm angry at myself. Why wasn't I here to protect her? She wanted me to feel comfortable in her world. She tried to please me. She slipped away from the media and her guards because she thought that it made me more comfortable, but it cost her life. At least, her guard could've protected her from that monster. The one time she lets him off is the one time she gets killed. I feel every bit responsible for her death. I may not have been there to protect her, but there's one thing I'm sure of; I'm going to fight for her."

They discussed the matter further. Jessica gathered information from Chad. She decided to investigate as much as she could without interfering with the police's investigation. Chad excused himself and headed home. As he was driving back to his place, he noticed a black Impala tailing him. He thought it was just a coincidence, so he brushed it off until he saw the car again on the next street. To ease his mind, he drove around for a few more minutes. The vehicle continued to follow him. He became suspicious. *"I wonder, is this Blaire's killer?"* He thought. He circled the block and pulled his white Jaguar over in front of his home. Much to his surprise, the police were already camped out in his driveway. A young black man dressed in a suit and tie was standing next to his vehicle as he exited. He handed Chad a legal document, and in a robotic, mundane voice, he said,

"Chadwick Lancaster, we have a warrant to search your property, including all your vehicles. Please step away from the vehicle sir."

Two officers escorted Chad to the living area of his home and asked him more questions. Chad was furious that they seemed to be focusing their attention on him rather than the real killer.

"What in the hell are you guys doing? You've got to be kidding me. This is a mistake. You know I didn't do this."

They placed him in the back of a police car and took him to the police station for thorough questioning. Hair and saliva samples were taken, as well as his fingerprints, which Chad was all too happy to give them, knowing he was innocent. After willfully submitting his DNA, he demanded to see his attorney. He felt he was being treated more like a suspect after being spoken to harshly by the investigating detectives. The only thing the police felt they had going in their favor was the possibility that Chad had no verifiable alibi for the exact time of her death. They focused on that for the time being. They couldn't formally charge him until the results of the DNA became available. He explained to them in detail that he was in Miami and had only chartered a flight the day he discovered her. After giving them Amanda's information, she verified that he had been in Miami but admitted that there was at least a twenty-four-hour window where he wasn't with her, and his whereabouts couldn't be verified.

Chad's attorney arrived at the police station and demanded his immediate release. The police immediately began putting together a timeline and focused on Chad's phone records, his flight information as well as the coroner's release of the time of death. Angry that the police suspected him, he called Jessica. He told her everything that happened.

"Now, do you see why I need your help? I was held for questioning for killing my fiancée. I was in Miami. I called her the morning of her death. After a while, the phone went dead, and I tried calling her back. When I didn't get an answer, I chartered a plane out of Miami.

They could've checked that information before they took me downtown. This makes absolutely no sense to me. My attorney told me not to worry about it, and I know I shouldn't, but if they can hold me for questioning in her death, what else are they capable of? I tried to tell them that I wasn't involved, but they wouldn't listen. It seems as if they were hell-bent on making me a killer."

"Who do you think could've done this, Chad?"

"I don't know," he said, looking aloof. "The police say there was no sign of forced entry, so she knew her killer. When I made it home, I noticed that the door was already unlocked when I began to place my key in the lock. When I saw her lying on the bed nude, I lost it. I can't remember much after that. She wasn't familiar with anyone in Little Rock. She was trusting of just about everyone. Whoever killed her must've appeared innocent enough that she chose to open the door for them. I'm the only one who knew she was there. When we were in Miami, a few photographers were following us around, taking pictures. Perhaps it was someone who's been keeping up with her from the tabloids. Who knows? There's no telling which sicko followed her back to my place. She could've had a stalker, someone from her past perhaps." Shaking his head out of confusion, he said, "I don't know what to think."

"I'll do some snooping around. I have friends in the police force. I'll get with them to see what I can find out, but as I said before, the police are capable of getting to the bottom of this." Chad didn't share her enthusiasm.

"I'm not confident in their ability to do so. That's why I called you. I'll pay you top dollar to solve this case for me."

"I'll do what I can. I'll call you if I find out anything." They ended their call.

Jessica called her contact at the police department to see what was happening on the case.

Chad went to his mother's home and talked with her. She was sitting in the dining area. She knew he was suffering. She had never seen her son in so much pain.

"How are you holding up son?" she asked. He lowered his head and sat next to her on the sofa.

"Mom, the police searched my vehicles, and they took me down to the police station for questioning. They finally let me go. I don't know what's going on, but this isn't right. I can see how an innocent person can be blamed for a crime they didn't commit. I have to tell you, Mom, I was afraid for the first time in my life. I've never been through anything like this before." He sobbed. His mother did her best to comfort him and encouraged him not to give up. She got up from her seat and placed her arms around him. His father heard the commotion, and he went in to help to comfort his son. His father said,

"You know we're here for you." He placed his hand on his shoulder.

"Thank you, dad. I love you both."

He hugged his parents and went to his car. He sat there thinking about Blaire's parents. They had to be experiencing far more grief than he was. He called her father while still sitting in his parent's driveway.

"Mr. Kensington, it's Chad. I'm calling to check on you. I want you to know I have someone looking into Blaire's death alongside the police."

Mr. Kensington said, "Son, I know you had nothing to do with the death of my daughter. I just know it. Justice will come in due time."

"How's Mrs. Kensington doing?"

"She's not doing well. Blaire was our world and now she's gone. Our family is broken. She was our greatest accomplishment. She was loving, beautiful, and so full of life. She could make you laugh regardless of what you were going through. She brought sunshine when she walked in your presence, and her smile was contagious. I tell you, Chad, I really have to question the big guy about this one. I don't see how we'll ever come back from this. My baby didn't deserve this. We've been robbed by one selfish, cowardly bastard."

"Mr. Kensington, I promise you when we find the person who did this, I'll stop at nothing to make sure he pays for what he's stolen from us." After talking a little more, they ended their call.

Nigel was in Miami. Almost every media outlet carried the story of Blaire's death which served as a constant reminder of his evil deed. He was severely distraught over his actions. He mourned her death. His mind constantly wandered. He thought he was in love with Blaire, and he was sure that he could convince her to love him. His plan failed, and he was unsure of his next move. In the past, he depended on Chad and his parents to rescue him when he was in trouble, but this was a problem he'd have to deal with all alone. Without family support, he grew increasingly unstable. He tried his best to stay under the radar, and he became distant day by day, living in fear that he would give himself away or that his secret would be revealed. Chad, on the other hand, was feeling the need to connect with his brother so he reached out to him. Nigel looked at the caller ID and saw it was Chad. He was reluctant to answer but he knew he had to in order to avoid suspicion.

"Hello"

"Hey, Nigel, What's up with you, bro?" Nigel, doing his best to keep his cool, said,

"Nothing much just relaxing. I have a couple of meetings in Little Rock this week, so I'll be headed back to Arkansas soon."

Chad said, "I want to see you when you get here. I really could use the company. I have a lot of unfinished business to attend to, but first, I must find the person who killed my fiancé, and when I do, I'm going to make him pay with his very life. I'm going to need my bro. I know you got my back." Nervously speaking, Nigel said,

"I want to help you in any way I can. Just let me know what you need." Out of curiosity, Nigel asked,

"Do they have any leads on a suspect?"

"Unfortunately, they don't. I'm the only one they're looking at. When this investigation is over, Blaire's real killer will be revealed." Nigel thought about what his brother had just said. The mere thought of his dirty deed being uncovered was enough to cause the bile to rise in his gut. He swallowed hard and became silent. For a moment, Chad thought the call had dropped.

"Hello, bro. Are you still there?" Clearing his throat Nigel pulled himself together. He said,

"Yeah, I'm here."

Chad asked, "Do you know what time you'll be back in Arkansas?"

"Not at the moment, but I'll let you know when I'm on my way."

"Sounds great, and bro, I love you man." Nigel went silent for a second.

"I, I love you too," he said quietly under his breath. He quickly ended the call. He sank into his seat. Feeling the total weight of the guilt, he so rightly deserved, he silently sobbed. He said out loud, *"What in the hell am I going to do? Nigel, you've really fucked up this time."* He collected his thoughts, remembering what Chad said about the case, how they had no other suspects. He said, *"They have nothing on me. Nobody saw me."*

He began to plan a strategy in the event he would be questioned by the police. But as far as he knew, nobody knew he had been in town, so he was feeling pretty confident. He created an alibi. He was going to tell them he was in Miami at the time. He took a flight later that week to Little Rock. He rented a car and went to his apartment downtown. He quickly went inside and closed his blinds. He checked his messages, read his e-mails, and tried to get a little sleep.

After about an hour of him being home, Chad called. They met at their parent's home. Nigel arrived before Chad. He went in to speak to his parents. His mother was sitting at the computer. He went over and kissed her on the cheek.

"Hello mother."

"Well look who's made it back in town. Are you here to stay for a while or are you going back to Miami?"

"I dunno mom. I haven't made up my mind yet. I need to see what the police have found out about the arson at my place. I haven't heard from them on the case. It's been almost a year and a half, and they still haven't arrested the woman who committed the crime."

"I'm sorry to hear that, sounds like you need to pick a better woman the next time. A good girl like your brother had. It's devastating what happened to that poor girl; may God rest her soul. I sure hope they find out who killed her. We don't need someone dangerous like that roaming the streets; and the nerve of the police to harass your brother."

Nigel didn't say much. He went to find his father. On his way to look for him, he noticed Chad had come. He tried to hurry out of the room, but Chad called out to him. He walked over and gave him a long brotherly hug. Nigel, feeling guilty, slowly pulled away.

"Hey there bro. What's up?"

"I'm good. I was just about to go and see Dad for a minute."

"Well, hold up a minute. I'll come with you."

Chad kissed his mother, and he and Nigel walked to the den.

"Hey, Pop," Nigel said, taking a seat across from him on the sofa.

"How are you, boys?" He asked.

They made small talk. Nigel focused more on his father as he was still a bit uneasy around his brother. He could sense the urgency of Chad wanting to speak with him alone and it made him nervous.

Finally, Chad said, "Come on, Nigel. Let's go and grab a bite to eat."

Nigel slowly shifted his eyes away from his father to Chad who was looking anxious. His jaw tightened. He slowly exhaled. He wanted to buy himself a little more time, but he knew it was useless. Although he was reluctant, he went. They took Chad's car and went for a drive. His brother wasted no time getting right to the point. The topic of discussion was Blaire, and Nigel was in no mood to talk about her. Chad gave him all the details he could think of, while his brother knew all too well what had taken place. His mind played over the crime scene as his brother continued to speak.

"I just don't understand it, Nigel. Why did she even have to open the door for them?"

He began beating his steering wheel out of frustration. Feeling that his brother was beginning to lose control and possibly causing an accident, Nigel asked,

"Do you want me to drive man?"

"No, man I got it. I'm just frustrated, that's all. I mean why would the police think I had something to do with this is beyond me. The detectives checked my alibi against the time of death, especially since I was the one who found her body. They're still researching all my information now. I called Jessica. She's going to help me with the case. I want her to find this fucker before the cops do because I'm going to have the pleasure of killing him myself. I'm going to choke the life out of him the same way he killed my Blaire. You wait and see."

Nigel gripped the passenger-side handle as Chad increased his speed, violently taking the Jaguar into the deep curves of the road.

"Man, you need to calm down and let the police handle this."

Chad frowned at him, "Man, they're already barking up the wrong tree. How am I supposed to believe they'll find the real killer when they're only focusing on me?"

"Look man, they'll get it all straightened out. It's customary for them to question the significant other in all murder cases where there is no clear killer."

"Nigel, they didn't just question me, they held me and wouldn't allow me to leave until I called my attorney. I sat in a locked interrogation room until he came. I had to submit a sample of my DNA. They took pictures of me, searched my vehicles, and took my fingerprints. I mean, they raked me over with a fine-tooth comb. I don't believe they're out looking for another killer. I bet they're trying to prove a case against me. While they are focusing on me, Jessica and I will be focusing on finding the real killer."

After a few minutes, they pulled up to the detective agency to chat with Jessica Barnes. When Nigel noticed they were at the agency he almost panicked. His nerves were on edge. His stomach began turning into knots. The churning of his bowels caused an uncomfortable ache within. Although nervous, he went inside. He tried to make good of the visit by convincing himself that perhaps it was a win for him. Using any information Jessica would share with Chad, he could stay a step ahead of the investigation. He'll know what's happening and if he must, he can divert any attention away from himself. They went inside. Jessica walked up to Chad and Nigel. Nigel tried to sit, but she stopped him, motioning for them to come back to her office.

"Hi, guys, what's up?"

"I just stopped by to see if you had anything yet," Chad said.

"Nothing yet." As they walked to her office, she looked over her shoulder a little focusing her attention on Nigel for a quick second.

"Hi, Nigel. Are you back for good?"

"I'm not sure yet. I'm gonna play it by ear. I have a few meetings this week and I want to check on the arson case." They finally stepped into her large posh office where they were seated.

"Chad, I haven't found anything yet. The police have this case wrapped up so tight that I can't seem to get close to it. Even my friends on the force have limited information because it's such a high-priority case. Only a select few people are allowed to go near it. Her father has sent his team of investigators here to make sure the police are doing everything they can to find the killer. They aren't even allowed in the loop. I spoke with the lead investigator, but at this time, they're all mum, and the only information I have is what they're giving to the public through the media. So as for now, my hands are tied."

Chad sank in his seat hearing the news. "So, Jessie what are we supposed to do, just sit around here on our fists and do nothing while the police department continues to botch up this case?"

"No, I wouldn't say that. The L.R.P.D. are the finest around. I have full confidence that they'll do everything in their power to get this case solved. In the meantime, I know the police are waiting to process the entire scene, looking for forensic evidence, fingerprints, you know, the usual. That's why they took DNA samples from you; they're ruling you out as a suspect. It seems cruel, and most innocent people are offended by it, but your cooperation with the authorities is crucial to the case. Once you're cleared, they can begin to look elsewhere."

Nigel wanted to cast off any suspicion, so he said, "Chad let the police do their job. They'll find this guy sooner or later." He looked over at Jessica and said, "Besides, with Jessica on the case she's bound to solve this before the police."

Jessica looked at Nigel and said, "I sure hope you're right about that." They all stood to their feet. She hugged Chad, then Nigel, and whispered in his ear,

"Take care of him and make sure he stays outta trouble." Nigel kissed her on the cheek and said,

"Don't worry, I will."

They left. Nigel drove instead. He took Chad to a sports bar where they ordered a bite to eat. He drank a few beers while Chad cried on his shoulders. He poured his heart out to Nigel. He went on and on about Blaire. He painted a glorious picture of her. Nigel was fond of her too. In a sick twisted sort of way, he longed to hear more about the woman he'd killed. His obsession for her went far beyond the grave. He listened to his brother's stories and after they were done eating, they left for Nigel's place. Chad didn't want to be alone, so Nigel put him in the spare bedroom, and they both went to bed; only Nigel lay awake thinking about Blaire. Wishing she was still alive, he was reminiscing about the moment she gave in to him, the moment when she thought he was Chad. He toyed with the idea that she must've known it was him instead. He was aroused thinking about the moments of sexual ecstasy they both shared. Lying on his back, he began to rub himself until he ejaculated. He went to sleep with her on his mind.

CHAPTER FOUR

Nigel was up before Chad. He was awakened by a noise outside. He stepped out onto his patio to look around, but he didn't see anyone. He went inside and showered. He put on a pot of coffee and turned the television on. The morning news programs were still covering the death of Blaire and the facts of the case. Nigel was pleased to hear there were no suspects. He quickly turned to another station. Chad, smelling the coffee, came out and went into the kitchen. He poured himself a cup and went to sit where Nigel was sitting.

"Hey man, what's up?"

"Nothing man, just sitting here channel surfing."

"Turn it to the news. I want to see what they're talking about."

"Look man, you already know what's on there. You shouldn't be watching that right now. It's only going to cause you more stress."

"Nigel man, nothing's worse than losing the love of my life. Our love is what fuels me to learn everything I can about her case. After that, then maybe I'll get some peace. Until then, I'm going to,"

…. Suddenly, a loud crash interrupted their conversation. Chad and Nigel both hit the floor as shards of glass sprayed the living room. They noticed a large brick had come through Nigel's window landing on the floor. There was a note attached. Chad went over and picked it up. He turned it over and read it. He looked at Nigel and said, "It's for you man." Nigel pursed his lips and snatched the brick out of Chad's hand. He took the rubber band off and read it. It read, *"It's not over, you whore; I know you think I forgot. Watch your back. I'm going to burn this motherfucker down too!"* He leaned back a little, and out of frustration, he said,

"Damn, I'm sick of this bitch! The police act as if they can't find her crazy ass. It's been a year since she set my shit on fire, and this motherfucking girl is still acting stupid. Shit, I thought she would've moved on with her life by now."

Chad realized he'd dropped his cup of coffee during the commotion. He got his cup that was still lying on the floor and cleaned up the spill. Afterward, he got dressed and intended to leave. When he got out of his car, he noticed that both of his brother's vehicles had been vandalized. The tires were slashed, and vulgar messages were etched into his paint and on his windows. He went back upstairs and got Nigel. Nigel was reluctant to call the police, so Chad made the call for him. After placing a police report, he called the towing service and had the vehicles towed to the dealership for repairs. Chad took him back to his parent's home, where he'd left his rental car the previous night. He continued driving it while his vehicles were being repaired. Chad went to the police station alone. He wanted to speak to someone on Blaire's case. He finally found the detective in charge of her case. His name was Byron Armstrong. The large, bold, white detective stood to his feet when he saw him walk into his office. "Have a seat, Mr. Lancaster," he said. The detective took his seat behind his desk. He was a little suspicious of Chad's visit. He wasn't sure if he was completely innocent, but he wasn't about to share any information with him. If anything, he wanted Chad to talk because he felt that something he would say could help him with his case.

"What can I do for you?" The detective tried to read his body language. He looked every bit the part of a grieving loved one. The detective thought either he was a very good actor, or he was truly grieving. He wasn't convinced either way.

"Have you found out anything about my fiancée?"

"Anything like what?" Chad was offended at the suspicious way the detective looked at him. With furrowed brows, he gave off a condescending expression that angered Chad. He knew the detective was still eyeing him as the killer.

"You think I'm guilty, don't you?" Almost in a smug kind of way the detective hunched his shoulders up and down with a fixed stare and said,

"Well, *are* you?"

"Un-fucking-believable! I don't know why I came down here. It's obvious that I'm wasting my time with you people. How could anyone ever think I could hurt her? I loved her."

"Mr. Lancaster, one thing has me puzzled about this case; it appears that the only person who knew your fiancée was in your home was you. Also, we can't find DNA from any other source other than yours inside of the victim. Although your flight information and phone records indicate you were on your way to Arkansas, the evidence says you were possibly here in time enough to commit the crime. How do you explain that? It's clear you two had sex right before her death, so tell me the truth. Did something happen while you two were making love? Did things get a little rough? You know it's been known to happen. All you have to do is tell me if it was an accident. We can work something out with the prosecuting attorney."

Chad lost all hope. He hung his head and cupped his hands over his face.

"You guys are never going to find her killer, are you? How many times do I have to tell you? I wasn't there! I'd have to be in two places at one time, and we both know that's impossible. My alibi checks out."

"Perhaps the time of death is a bit off. It's been known to happen. The medical examiner gave an estimated time of death, so there's still a strong possibility that you would've been able to commit this crime."

Chad stood to his feet and leaned his body over Detective Armstrong's desk. The detective leaned forward to let him know he would not be intimidated by whatever it was he was about to say. Chad whispered desperately,

"Detective, have you ever lost someone that you truly loved? I mean, you loved them so deeply that you couldn't live your life without them. Someone who you'd gladly give your life for to live happily in this world, even if it means living it without you. Well, I have. Blaire was that special someone for me. I would give my life for her just so she could come back, live, love, and simply smile again because she deserves that. This world lost a beautiful person, and it won't be the same without her in it. She should still be alive, and you're right; I'm as much to blame as the sick, twisted bastard who took her away. I failed her because I wasn't there to protect her. The only thing that's even remotely keeping me afloat is finding her killer. If you do anything in this world, I pray that you, for once, take the focus off of me and try to find out who did this. Now, I know you must do your job and focus on me, but I'm begging you: please give me peace before I die. Find her killer for me." Tears streamed down his face. His lips trembled as he spoke.

"All I want is justice for Blaire." The hardened detective swallowed the lump in his throat. He looked Chad over. He was very convincing. He reached into his desk and found a box of tissues. He plucked a few from the box and handed them to Chad.

"Mr. Lancaster, we *will* find her killer."

"Thank you, detective." Detective Armstrong's face was red. He almost felt a sense of guilt for bringing Chad to the brink of a breakdown. He stood to his feet and walked around the other side of his desk where Chad was standing.

"This is an ongoing investigation, and we'll promptly give any new updates on this case per department policies to her next of kin. Even then, we wouldn't be able to share some information due to the nature of the case. We wouldn't want the *real killer* to know we're on to him. I hope you understand." The detective lifted his eyes, focusing on the words "Real Killer," letting Chad know he sympathized with him without officially saying so, which gave him hope.

"I understand," he said. "Thank you, Detective Armstrong. He left.

He called Jessica to inform her about his visit to the police station. After speaking with her, he went to his parents' home.

The media had been calling the Lancaster family for an exclusive story since Blaire's death, and for the most part, they were able to avoid them. Still, they continued to get pesky so Chad, who wanted to take advantage of the opportunity to find the killer with the public's help, allowed himself to be interviewed. He promised to speak with them if they didn't harass his parents. Everyone was quiet as he made his statement.

"I'm determined now more than ever to find the person who committed this crime. I want to know who took my beautiful lady from me, from her family. I only hope the police find him before I do. My parents are here to support me in my time of grief, and they, too, are devastated. we ask you to sincerely consider giving us privacy and time to grieve during this difficult time in our lives."

Immediately, he was bombarded with more questions from reporters like, "*Who do you think could have done this? Where were you when it happened? Why did the police question you? Are you considered a suspect at this time?*" The questions went on and on. Chad answered as many as he could. He finally was able to push through them. He went inside and made plans to take his parents to a more peaceful environment until things could blow over. He found his mother, who was watering her plants.

"Mom, I think you and Dad need to go somewhere else because these reporters will not let up." His mom put one of her hands on her hip and said,

"I'm not about to let anybody run me from my home. I'm staying put."

"Mom, it's just until all of this blows over. Blaire was very popular, and she lived her life in the spotlight. The tabloids had been following her for years. They're ruthless people, and they'll do anything to get a story, even harass your loved ones and go through your trash. They'll hunt you down. Some of their behavior is just downright disturbing."

His mother said, "Now that goes to show you that they'll find us no matter where we go, so we may as well stay here. They can sit there all day as long as they stay out there and don't come on private property. We're not intimidated. If they want to sit out there, let them. They'll get tired and go home soon enough."

His father agreed. He knew there would be no reasoning with his parents, so he gave up. He didn't want to be alone, so he stayed with them.

In the meantime, Nigel was having troubles of his own. He went to his home and grabbed some clothes. He placed a large suitcase on the bed and began packing.

He was startled by a familiar but disturbing voice. He looked up from packing and noticed in the shadows there stood the silhouette of a curvy figure. She wore black leather shorts, leather boots up to her thighs, a leather bra, and a choker set with rhinestones. She had a long, black, wavy wig that went all the way to her buttocks. She wore fishnet stockings.

"Hello Nigel, my love. Are you going somewhere?"

Shocked to see who it was calling out to him, he gripped his chest out of fear.

"Bitch! How in the fuck did you get in here? What are you doing here?" Tilting her head slightly, she looked at him and said,

"I missed you baby. That's why I'm here." She held out her arms and said, "I'm wearing your favorite outfit. Don't you want to fuck me, baby?" He noticed she had a small handgun in her right hand. He was angry, but more so, he was nervous.

"Danielle, you need to leave before I call the police on your crazy ass. I already have a restraining on you."

"Oh baby, they didn't tell you? That ole thing expired."

"Well, that's not a problem. I'll get another one, and we'll add vandalism, and breaking and entering to your list of crimes."

"Now baby, why would you want to have me arrested? If I'm in jail, you won't get any of this good lovin' you said you love so much. You know, I'm the woman you said you were going to marry. I have a list of broken promises from you. Because of your promises, I quit my job and sold my home to relocate here to Little Rock and work for you. You told me we were going to be married. I uprooted my mother, who was very ill. I moved her away from the only home she knew. I still believe she died of a broken heart. After her death, you began treating me differently. Soon after, you initiated a minor argument with me to break things off and you left me without warning. What did I do to deserve that? It would've been better if you would've just told me the truth before allowing me to uproot my life. Then you discarded me like a piece of trash. I gave up everything to be with you, and you gave me nothing in return. The way I see it, since my mother lost her home and I lost mine, I'm figuring a house for a house. I'm going to burn this bitch down too! It's a shame, too, because it's such a lovely home."

"Bitch, you've lost your damn mind. Do you think I'm going to sit here and let you burn my shit down?" She lifted the gun and pointed it at him.

"It looks as if you have no choice in the matter. I did it before, and I'll do it again." She waved the gun at him and said, "Now sit your bitch ass on the bed. I want to talk to you. I've got questions, and I need answers."

He refused to be seated. His phone rang, and he asked, "Are you going to let me take this call?"

She laughed at him and said, "What do you think? Throw it on the floor right next to my feet. If you try anything stupid, I swear I'll fuck you up." He slowly pulled the phone out of his pocket and pressed the call button as he was doing so. He threw it at her feet and yelled out loud,

"Danielle, please don't shoot me!" He hoped the caller on the other end heard him and would send help. She picked up the phone and answered, but nobody was on the line.

"They must've had the wrong number."

She took the phone and placed it on the floor, crushing it with the heel of her boot. "Now, we don't have to worry about anyone disturbing us. Nigel, honey, I just want to talk." She motioned for him to sit on the bed to listen to her. He eased down on the bed and kept his eyes on the gun. As she spoke, he tried to hatch a plan of escape.

"When you broke it off with me, you cut me off cold without any warning or explanation. When you woke that morning, you were in a bad mood. I asked you what was wrong, and you said you didn't want to discuss the matter. You began yelling at me, went into the bathroom, closed the door, and asked me to leave. I never heard from you again. After many attempts to contact you, I finally saw you with another woman and we had words. Do you remember that? Yeah, I think you do. You called me names in front of your other whore. Names I didn't deserve. I tried to wrap my mind around what was happening but couldn't. What I want to know is why? I want answers, and I feel I deserve them. So, Mr. Playboy, what do you have to say for yourself?" He saw the pain he caused and the direct ramifications of his actions for the first time, but he still didn't care. He didn't want to tell her the truth, so he tried to weasel his way out of it with the, *"I don't know"* statement. She lifted the gun and pointed it at his head.

"I want answers, asshole! This time, I need the truth."

"If I tell you the truth, you're going to kill me."

"Let me hear it. Considering the shit I've been through; you may as well tell me."

"Well, okay; since you want to know, here it is. I did like you in the beginning. I enjoyed you, and I loved being around you. Each time you fucked me, I wanted more. I liked you alright, but you began pressuring me every day wanting me to commit. Your pussy was so good, and man, the way you sucked my dick, it was like nothing I'd ever felt before. A guy will say anything when you're sucking him right. Yeah, I said I wanted to marry you. Did you ever notice that the only time I mentioned marriage, was during sex? The more I mentioned it, the better the sex got. I never thought you were going to get serious about it. When you said you were going to move closer to Little Rock, I thought it was cool; that way, I could have sex with you any time I wanted instead of having to pay to bring you here. So I gave you a little position within my company; where was it in the mail room?" He provided an evil smirk and continued.

"I never told you to sell your mom's property. You did a lot of that shit on your own. Before I knew it, you had moved here with your mother. After she died, you became clingy. You were always at my place, and I felt smothered. I wasn't ready for all of that. I didn't know how to tell you without hurting your feelings, so yeah, I started an argument with you to break it off. Now that's the real truth."

"Nigel, it would've been better if you would've told the truth from the beginning. I would've been broken-hearted, but I would've gotten over it, but to allow me to uproot my life was way too much. You never thought about me. You were too selfish."

He interrupted her. "Danielle, we never really did anything together but have sex. That's all we had in common. I know you saw that coming. Every dinner led to sex. Every date led to sex; no matter what we did, it always led us right back to the bedroom. Hell, I only met your mother once. Didn't that tell you something? Damn! A lot of times, y'all women blame us men for your wishful thinking. Sometimes y'all need to open your fucking eyes. How do you move your entire life for a relationship based solely on sex? Now you want to get mad and, in your feelings, by burning my shit down and fucking up my property. What real self-respecting woman does that? You had no engagement ring from me and no real proposal, only sexual promises. Now who's to blame?"

She got angry and said, "You are you fucking bastard. Don't try to turn the tables on me, you selfish mother-fucker. That's why I want to kill you, but I won't, at least not right now. The thing is, I still loved you; I never learned how to let that go. You see, I don't take rejection too well." He looked at her and said in a sarcastic tone,

"Wait, don't tell me, daddy issues?" He laughed to hurt her feelings.

"No motherfucker. It's men like you who think you can play with women's feelings. Yeah, y'all motherfuckers are so smooth with your shit that y'all even have women hating each other and fighting one another over you none deserving assholes. I could've fucked your whores up long ago, but I knew they may have been under the same spell I was under. There was no sense in fighting them because my problem wasn't with them. My issues were with you!"

"I didn't tell you to fall in love with me. I gave you some good dick and you couldn't handle it, face it. Deal with it and move on like everybody else."

"I'm going to move on, but I'm going to make you pay first. You're going to pay me back for all my troubles."

"Hmm. How so?" He wanted to get into her head so that he could crush what was left of her self-esteem. He began degrading her, commenting on her appearance.

"Look at you wearing that outfit. It looks sexy on you. You're getting my dick hard just by looking at you in it. You know what to wear to get a rise out of me. That's the only time I could get my dick up for you until you sucked me off with those big-ass thick lips of yours. You look like a whore, and whores get my dick hard because they are willing to do anything sleazy to get me off. That's why I loved to see you wearing shit like that. I would never ask any woman that I planned to marry to dress that way. Any woman who wants to be my wife must have boundaries. A real man loves a woman who has boundaries, a woman with restraints, and who knows how to tell a man, "Hell No," when she knows he's full of shit. You see, we men tend to do what we can get away with. What a woman will allow us to do. If I can talk you into doing anything degrading for me, then I don't want you, at least not to marry. You must have self-love. If a man requests something that goes against your convictions, you should tell him you won't do it. I played you like a puppet. You swallowed my dick and all for the promise of marriage. You did everything I told you. You even blew my ass, which, by the way, was sort of strange. I never had a bitch do that before. You were my first. After that, you received no more kisses from me. That's just nasty. You were nothing more than a tool. What will your next man think of you? How can you stand at the altar and kiss your new husband with the same mouth you tossed my salad with? Yuck. Oh, and your children, guess what type of mouth is going to kiss them goodnight. Now tell me the truth, did you do all those filthy things because you enjoyed them, or did you do them because you thought that's what I wanted? If you say you did it because of me, then you have your answer. Hell, I lost respect for you when you lost respect for yourself. If you lose a guy because you won't degrade yourself, it's not a loss. Real men marry good women, women with values and standards who can be trusted. We come back and fuck women like you all on a promise. Learn the difference, and maybe somebody will marry your pathetic ass in the future."

She smiled and said, "Say what you will, asshole. The things you say don't bother me, but you're going to pay me."

"Pay you for what?"

"I want you to pay me for my losses. For starters, I want to buy my mother's home back and live a lavish lifestyle just like you."

She was getting tired from standing on her feet, so she said, "Stand up and let's go into the other room. I want to take a seat; these shoes are hurting my feet." She walked him into the living room. They were both seated, and she got her purse, which was already in the room. She had it hidden behind the throw pillows on the sofa. She reached inside and pulled out a disc. She tossed it to him. "Why don't you pop that in the player so we can see what we're dealing with here?" He did as she told him. She placed her gun in her lap and told him a story.

"I've been watching you for a year and a half now. I've been watching every move you made from Miami to Arkansas and back again. Guess what I stumbled upon?" Out of curiosity, his eyes were glued to the screen; he watched the footage while she relaxed on the sofa. "You see where this is going, don't you?" She placed her gun on the table. She was so confident that she went into the kitchen and fixed herself a glass of wine while he continued to watch the video. When she came back, his eyes were still fixed on the screen.

"I know I tend to be a bit psychotic and all, or as you put it, *"low self-esteem,"* but I was in love. I thank you for schooling me. You were very convincing in getting me to believe you really cared about me. I have to admit, I was obsessed with you. I presumed you to be a real catch. I prayed to God that I could turn my back on this situation and forgive you, but as you say, my self-esteem and my daddy issues wouldn't allow me to let it go. Since we've both established that I'm psychotic and un-stable, there's no telling what I'm willing to do to your black ass. Perhaps you'll think twice before hurting any-one else. I've been following you closely. You may call it stalking, but hey, there's a fine line. Animals stalk their prey, and then after toying with it, they kill it. I'm no animal. That's a title more befitting of you. I placed a GPS tracker on your vehicles and a locator on your cell phones. I knew where you were going to be before you knew it. I have friends in many places, and I'm far more intelligent than you give me credit. You really shouldn't sleep so soundly. I could've killed you long ago. I've been in and out of here more times than you know. Shit, I even laid next to you a couple of times while you slept. Before I burned down your little fuck spot, I used to go there and watch you sleep. Oh, how I contemplated kill-ing you. When you moved to Miami, I flew over, too. I even have an apartment there. It's not as fancy as your brother's condo or your new place. I've made it a full-time job of watching you. Guess what? I know where you were when Blaire Kensington was killed. Speaking of stalking, you were so busy stalking her that you never noticed me. I followed you from Miami. Every stop you made, I made. Every fuel station you stopped at, I was there. I can't see how we both made that trip without sleep. I thought for sure you would stop and get a room, but that never happened. I know you killed her. Don't believe me? Keep on watching the screen. I watched from the large glass slider. After you raped and murdered her, I hid in the brush as you came running out crying. I then followed you back to Miami. I was even at the funeral. There's footage on there. I've been watching your every move. I have a library of footage on you. Never underestimate the power of a woman. Do you know how many of your female employees you've fucked? It seems you've slept with almost half the women who work for you, and it looks as if you've managed to cause them to hate you. Actually, that's not the word most of them use to describe their feelings for you. It was more like they loathed you." She walked over to him and began to massage his shoulders.

"Before you go trying to kill me to keep me quiet, I want you to know I have an insurance plan in place. In the event of my untimely demise, I have hours of footage and other evidence that will immediately be sent to the police, the media, and your family. It still bothers me watching you stalk that poor woman, throwing yourself at her. While your brother was in Miami, you were right here in Arkansas killing his fiancée. I see not only do you not care about women; you don't even care about your own blood." Nigel was stunned. He couldn't believe what he was hearing, but right there in his face was all the evidence; she had plenty of footage and still photos. It was unmistakable; it was him. As she massaged his shoulders, he was annoyed, so he removed her hands.

"What do you want Danielle?"

"I'm not about to put all my cards on the table today, but I can tell you this: I want to buy back my mother's home. I'll need some money for that immediately because the property is up for sale."

He got nasty with her and said, "You ought to have that in the bank. How much could that property be worth? It was in....where are you from again, Brinkley? Helena? Hell, I can't remember. I know it was one of those small hick towns. I mean the property couldn't be worth much in that country ass place. I might have that in my pocket. What's it worth two, three thousand dollars?"

She returned to her seat. "Your jokes don't bother me. As long as I make you pay, I'm okay. Keep watching the video; there's more." He came across some still footage of her holding a baby.

"Whose kid is that in the picture?"

"I'm so glad you asked. She's mine. Wait, let me rephrase that, she's ours. Too bad she's going to grow up without her daddy. But don't worry I'm going to see to it that she doesn't have daddy issues because you're going to provide for her. She's the real reason I'm doing this. If you don't believe anything I'm saying, I'm always available for a paternity test."

For a moment, he fixed his eyes on the baby in the still photos. She looked exactly like him. The baby was laughing in some of the footage. Her smile reminded him of his mother. It tugged at his heart. Danielle got her purse and boots and began to walk out without saying anything more. He yelled out to her,

"Danielle, where are you going? Can we talk about this?"

She ignored him. He called her name once more. She walked out of the door and slammed it behind her. He ran to the door and opened it. "Danielle, can we talk?" She continued to walk away without looking back. He stood still and watched as she walked down the street and got into her vehicle. Not wanting to embarrass himself, he went back inside. He felt defeated. He punched a hole in the wall out of frustration. He went back over to the television and looked at the video again. He knew he was doomed. He was still surprised about the news of having a daughter. He stared at her over and over. Seeing his daughter on the screen, he almost had a bout of decency and felt a small sense of remorse for hurting Danielle. He didn't know she was pregnant. Had he known, he would've wanted to be in his child's life even if he didn't love the mother. Still, that didn't negate the fact that she knew everything, and not only that, but she also had video footage to prove it. He had no clue of what to do next.

He sat back on his sofa and tried to come up with a plan, but he couldn't think of anything. He concluded there was nothing left to do but go along with Danielle's plan, at least for the time being.

CHAPTER FIVE

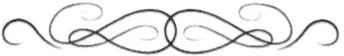

Chad decided it was time to go back to his place so he could come to grips with his pain and start the healing process. He had been so angry and focused on trying to find out more about Blaire's death that he hardly took any time to grieve properly. He was a little nervous as he put his key in the lock to turn it. For a moment, he toyed with the idea of opening the door, and Blaire would be there waiting for him. But he quickly realized after walking inside. He slowly walked in. During the investigation, his place had been gone over meticulously, and everything was in disarray. He went into his bedroom. The top mattress had been removed from his bed. Seeing the place where Blaire was lying when he found her, he just stood there for a while, staring in disbelief and trying to calm the pain. A few minutes had gone by when his doorbell rang. Looking through the window, he could see it was Jessica Barnes. Since the door was open, she stepped inside.

"How did you know I was here?"

"I called Mom, and she told me. She's at your parent's place. They're heading to their fitness class. I thought I'd stop by to check on you."

She looked around and asked, "Looks like they did a thorough job of going through this place. Is this your first time back?"

"Yeah, I just walked in the door before you came."

"When are you planning on cleaning? You know you can hire a professional cleaning service to do it for you if you don't feel up to it. There are a lot of great companies; you can look them up."

"No! I don't want strangers coming here. I can't ask my regular housekeeper to do it. I'll do it myself." Jessica began walking around and picking things off the floor. Latex gloves, foot covers, and other things were strewn about, mostly trash leftover from the investigation.

"I'll help you clean." Jessica didn't want him to be alone, especially since it was his first visit back inside the home since the event.

"Thanks."

They began cleaning each room. Chad went to find sheets to put on the box spring and made it look presentable until he could have a new bed delivered. Once he was done, he sat at the foot of the bed. He looked towards the walk-in closet. He went inside. Blaire's clothing was still there. She had unpacked her things and hung them on one side of the closet next to his. Tears began to pool in his eyes. Smiling through tears, he gathered her garments and held them in his arms. He noticed among some of her dresses just over to the left was a gift-wrapped box he didn't recognize. It looked as though it may have contained a watch. Jessica walked in as he was looking at it.

"Was it a present for her?"

"No, I've never seen it before now. It looks like something she planned on giving me. She said she had a surprise for me, but she never told me what it was. I guess this is it. It must be a fancy new watch." He smiled, thinking about her. "That's just like her, always thinking of others." Jessica wanted to leave him alone so he could have the moment to himself.

"I'll leave you alone. I'll be in the kitchen cleaning."

"No, you don't have to. I'm okay. I'd rather you stay." He slowly pulled the silver wrapping off the box while she looked on.

As he opened the box, he was perplexed by what he saw. Expecting to see a watch or bracelet, he thought the little gift was very odd. Jessica was no stranger to the gift. She knew exactly what it was.

"Is that what I think it is?" Jessica asked. She walked over to take a closer look and noticed the test was positive. "Chad, I think Blaire was pregnant." He stood with his mouth open and took a few steps back.

"Blaire was pregnant! That was the news she had for me. I was going to be a father. Jessica, we were going to be parents." He yelled out in pain. He became hysterical. Jessica tried calming him. After a while, she was able to get him to take a seat. She fixed him a shot of bourbon and talked to him calmly and soothingly. She felt bad for him. She was more determined to get to the truth for his sake. She stayed with him for a while. After he went to sleep, she called the detective in charge of the case and informed them that Blaire was pregnant. The detectives already knew she was pregnant, but they didn't tell the family. Jessica slipped out and went to the agency for a while. She called her former Lieutenant, Gary Fitz and spoke with him. He normally shares little tidbits with her from time to time. He informed her that a small tip of a pinkie finger's print was taken from Blaire's cell phone but couldn't be identified. He also told her there was DNA, but they were still searching. However, the DNA found inside Blaire seemed to be a match for Chad.

She wondered who could've handled the cell phone and why was Chad's semen in her at the time of her death when he reported he wasn't in town. It all sounded so strange to her. Things simply didn't add up. She wanted to know more but knew they wouldn't tell her anything. Why would Blaire open the door for someone she didn't know? She was thinking along the lines of a possible repairman or a delivery person, but the police ruled out all of that. She tapped her pencil against her desk, trying to think of any little clue that could help her.

Nigel went to visit his parents. While there, his mother made him lunch, and they sat at the dining room table and talked for a while. After visiting with her, he left for the office. As he pulled out of the driveway, he noticed a few photographers out front. They blocked his car. Angered by them, he got out and began yelling at them. Perceiving him to be Chad, they bombarded him with questions while snapping photos, hoping they would be granted an exclusive interview. Nigel, not the one for holding in his anger, threatened them with bodily harm if they wouldn't move their vehicles. He began berating them and yelling epithets. They saw the expression on his face and knew he was serious, so they backed off. He explained to them that he was Nigel, not Chad, and he wouldn't be answering any of their questions. He got back in his vehicle and slammed the door. As he gunned his engine, his tires burned rubber and left a cloud of smoke as he was leaving the home. Everyone was running, trying to get out of his way. Photographs and video footage of Nigel were taken. Stories began surfacing that he was Chad's identical twin brother. Reporters began scrambling, trying to find out more about him. Looking at the local news, homicide detective Byron Armstrong leaned closer to the TV to hear more about the story. He couldn't believe how much Nigel and Chad looked alike. Staring at the TV, he said out loud,

"Will you look at this shit? Well, I'll be damned, twins! Most identical twins share the same DNA. Let's see what we can find out about you, Mr. Nigel Lancaster."

He immediately got on the phone and called his office. Nigel's angry outburst at the reporters was quite interesting to this keen-nosed homicide detective. He had met Chad, and he was a gentle and kind soul. But this guy he saw on TV, had a scary side to him. He looked like the kind of guy you wouldn't want to get into a brawl with. He thought about the evidence. This new information about having an identical twin brother could turn this investigation in a whole new direction. He immediately began investigating Nigel. Where was he on the night of the murder? He knew Jessica was close to the family, so he called her for a quick chat. In the meantime, new details began to surface, and it was reported that Nigel was unaccounted for during the time of Blaire's death, but there was no evidence of him flying into town. Although they wanted to subpoena his phone records and get information on his credit cards, they couldn't obtain that information without a warrant, and they needed probable cause to obtain one. He wasn't a suspect at the time, but they were interested in him.

Jessica filled Detective Armstrong in on all she knew about the brothers. She told him that Nigel was the aggressor of the two men. Chad was a mild-mannered guy, and Nigel was arrogant and hostile. She shared her suspicion with him. She also shared that their families were very close, their mothers were best friends, and they had to tread carefully when accusing him. It could cause feuding and unrest between both families if they were wrong. Except for the fingerprint on the phone, no other evidence at the scene pointed to an unknown assailant.

Snooping Around

Curious to know how the case was going, Nigel decided to stop by the Barnes Detective Agency to see if Jessica was making progress in her investigation. Her mother, Mrs. Annette Barnes was there too. He walked in with confidence. After charming both ladies, *well at least believing he had,* he took a seat. Jessica, armed with the suspicion of his whereabouts and his unexpected visit, asked,

"What brings you by Nigel?"

He crossed one leg over the other and leaned back in his chair.

"I'm here for Chad. As you know, he hasn't been the same since all this happened. I love him, and I'm concerned about him. He's taking this so hard. I'm curious. Have you heard anything yet? I mean, since you *are* on the case."

"What would you like to know?"

She asked out of curiosity. She was on to him, but she decided to allow him to lay his cards on the table to see what type of hand he was playing.

"Well, what's going on? Have you guys or the police found any evidence, or has anything new come up?"

"I was with your brother the other day. We found out Blaire was pregnant, so when the killer is found, they'll be charged with the death of the unborn child as well."

Jessica was, in a sense, toying with him, giving him this information. Nigel was stunned to hear the news. His heart stopped for a minute and immediately began to beat rapidly. He thought, *"What have I done?"* He was visibly shaken at the news. The blood drained from his face. Jessica noticed the unsettling look in his eyes.

"Are you okay Nigel?" She asked. He shook it off and said,

"Umm....yeah, I'm okay. Are you sure she was pregnant?"

"Yes, I'm sure. You were going to be an uncle."

Nigel thought about his brother and then his parents. He realized his actions, and for a moment, he felt ashamed. The feelings of guilt had returned, but not the kind of guilt that made him want to confess and he had nothing to gain by doing so. Not only would he go to prison, but if found out, he would be hated by everyone. His friends and family would disown him. He would lose his business and any hopes of a relationship with his daughter. He would be destroyed forever. He raped Blaire, then killed her and her unborn child, and to make matters worse, someone knew about it. That someone could destroy him. He needed to get with Danielle. He needed to make sure she never spoke of this to anyone.

His cool, calm demeanor was replaced with fear, anxiety, and panic. He jumped to his feet and said, "Jessie, I gotta go!" He ran for the door and left without saying another word to Jessica. His behavior disturbed her. She looked at her mother and asked,

"What do you make of that?" Her mom shrugged her shoulders and said, "Maybe he was upset because a baby was murdered, and he realized he's not going to be an uncle."

"Yeah, I'm not getting that. When have you ever known Nigel to care about anyone but himself? He's always been cocky and arrogant. I mean, he and Chad are like night and day. I always felt he had narcissistic tendencies and he's a bit of a sociopath. He's like the evil of the two. He's taking the news rather hard for it to be an unborn child don't you think?" Her mother shook it off.

"I don't know. I guess." Her mother went back to work. Jessica leaned back in her chair.

"Mom, you're always at Mrs. Lancaster's home; where was Nigel when Blaire was killed? Was he in Arkansas?"

"No, he was in Miami. He was living with Chad out there for a brief time until he found his own place. Some woman was trying to kill him. She set fire to his place. Last I heard, Deloris said the police were still looking for her. Since the police couldn't find her, he decided to stay in Miami. As far as anyone knows, he was in Miami when Chad's fiancée was killed, and he's been there the entire time. He's been very supportive ever since all this happened.

"Who was running Lancaster Logistics while Nigel was in Miami?"

"I'm not sure. The business was in trouble until Chad pumped some money into it. I do remember being told that Chad didn't want Nigel to run it in the ground again, so he hired someone to oversee it. From what I'm told, Nigel and Chad basically collect money while others run the company. I think they have quarterly meetings they attend but that's about it." Jessica thought for a moment. She had a nagging feeling. She wanted to know who this woman was who was suspected of setting Nigel's place on fire. She had to be dangerous if she had Nigel running for his life.

In the meantime, Nigel had a phone call to make. His call was to Danielle. If he was going to get anywhere with her, he knew he needed to use a kind approach. He needed her in his corner. He wanted her to believe in him once more. He also wanted to meet his daughter. He felt guilty about having a daughter when he was responsible for killing his brother's child. He called Danielle; he waited nervously as the phone rang. It took so long for her to answer that he almost ended the call until he heard the voice on the other end.

"Hello," she said.

"Hello Danielle." As soon as she heard Nigel's voice she was alarmed.

"What is it, Nigel?"

"I want to know if we can talk. I'd like to meet with you."

"About what, Nigel?"

"I think we need to talk about our daughter. I'd like to meet her."

"Oh, *now* you're interested all of a sudden."

"I just learned about my daughter the other day. Of course, I'm interested. What type of man do you think I am? I know I may be an asshole when it comes to relationships. I've made many mistakes when dealing with you, and I have my reasons for my actions, reasons of which you may not understand, but I draw the line when it comes to children."

Still not impressed, she asked again, "So what do you want?"

"I told you I want to see you; I want to meet my daughter, our daughter." There was a long pause on the other end of the phone.

"Look if this is some sort of trick, you really need to stop. I can't handle any more games from you. Besides, I know your secret. How do I know I'll be safe?"

"Danielle, what you saw was an accident. It wasn't supposed to happen the way it did. I would like to explain it to you. You've got to trust me!"

"No, you lost my trust long ago." He pleaded with her for about ten minutes. He softened her up enough to get her to hear him out and eventually convinced her to come to his place.

"What time do you want me to come over?"

"Anytime," he said. She took a few minutes to think about it.

"Are you sure about that?"

"Yes, I'm sure."

"Just meet me there."

She ended the call without a word. He began to worry. Thinking he'd offended her in some way, he sat in his car with his head hanging low. He finally proceeded to his home. He went inside. After a couple of minutes, his doorbell rang. He opened the door. There Danielle stood waiting to come inside. In her arms was a cute little bundle dressed in all yellow. Her hair was soft and curly. He couldn't see her face. He invited her inside while helping her with her bags. She stood in the middle of the living area. He wanted to see the baby's face for himself. He anxiously waited. The baby had been asleep. She turned around to check her surroundings and looked into her father's eyes. She was a friendly baby, and she gave him the brightest smile. She looked exactly like his mother. He smiled at her; his heart melted.

He reached out for her. She willingly went to him. He began to talk to her. "Hello, there little princess. How are you? You are so beautiful." The baby smiled at him, showing her tiny little teeth. Her bright eyes sparkled, and she was in a playful mood. He held her closer to him. She smelled delicate, like baby powder. He was overcome with emotions as she reached out to him with her soft hand and touched his face.

"Why didn't you tell me about her?"

"I didn't think you'd want to know her. That's why I came to you the way I did."

"What's her name?"

"Miracle," her name is Miracle Denise. The name Denise is after my mom. There were many nights I sat thinking of terminating the pregnancy, but I felt it would be wrong, and it went against everything I believed in. Then, at the time of delivery, I almost lost her. She's a miracle. She almost didn't make it, but she fought hard. That's why I'll do everything within my power to protect her and her future at all costs. I've taken drastic measures that will ensure that if anything happens to me, the truth will come out. You've hurt me; I won't allow that to happen to my baby." He drew in a long, deep breath, smelling her hair, and said, "Miracle Denise Lancaster." Danielle said,

"She doesn't have your last name. You weren't there to sign the birth certificate, so I gave her my maiden name, Turner."

He looked at her in all sincerity and said, "Danielle I'm truly sorry. Whatever I can do to make this right, I will. I promise."

"We know what your promises are worth Nigel. I don't want my daughter getting caught up in your empty promises."

"She's our daughter," he said. He looked at the baby, "Look at those big pretty eyes. You look just like your grandmother. Do you want to meet Grandma? We've got to let her see you."

"I don't think that's such a good idea right now," she said.

"Why not? She needs to meet her family."

"Maybe now is not a good time. Perhaps we need to take things a little slower."

"Look; just because I've been an asshole doesn't mean you should punish her or my family. Allow her to meet her family. Her grandmother will be thrilled and so will her grandfather." He held the baby up and began to play with her. Danielle, looking on, wondered what his angle was. He seemed sincere, but Nigel is known to be selfish. She played along for a while to see where it would lead. After about an hour of visiting, he said, "I want her to have my last name. I'll sign the birth certificate; anything I must do, I will. I want her to meet my parents today. Would you like to ride over there with me?" Surprisingly she said yes.

He called ahead and told his mother he was bringing a visitor. He didn't tell her what was going on; he just asked that she and his father be there. They drove over to his parent's place. The ride was uneasy for Danielle. As they proceeded down the highway, she began to think of all the times she dreamed that she and Nigel were together raising their daughter. Her wish seemed to be coming true, but it felt fraudulent. Nigel chatted while they rode on. He was so chatty she'd almost wished he would be quiet so she could think.

Things were moving too fast for her. She began to get a little nervous. Her mind played over how he had killed Blaire. She began to feel that she was putting herself and her daughter in harm's way. She had the urge to get out of the car at the first sign of safety, but as she looked up, she realized they were heading towards his parent's neighborhood. She was no stranger to the home. She'd been there many times before when she was stalking him but now, she was being invited by him. There were a few reporters out, but Nigel quickly drove past them. After pulling into the long, winding driveway, they finally made it to the home. He gently took the baby out of her car seat as Danielle got the baby's bag. He proudly went inside. His parents were in the living room. He went inside and spoke to them. He introduced Danielle to his parents.

"Mom, Dad, I would like for you to meet someone. This is Danielle Turner. These are my parents." She shook their hands and said,

"It's very nice to meet you both." His mother looked at the baby Nigel was holding. She could tell this was her granddaughter without them having said a word.

"Nigel, who's this little one right here?" He turned her towards his mother and said,

"Mom, this is Miracle Denise Lancaster. Meet your granddaughter." She reached for the baby.

"Nigel, what have you done? Oh, my Lord, she is so beautiful. She has a head full of pretty hair. Come here, sweetheart." She held the baby and she and Nigel's father turned their attention toward the baby. "Honey, she looks just like you. She has your eyes," said Nigel's father.

"Yeah, Dad, she looks just like mom." The baby got a little fussy over all the attention and her strange sur-roundings, so Danielle reached for her. As soon as she was safe in her mother's arms, Nigel's mother reached out and popped Nigel on the back of the head with an open hand.

"Boy, how long have you known about this and kept it from us?" His parents began fussing at him. Danielle thought it was a bit comical watching Nigel get scolded like a teenage boy, and the expression on his face was priceless. At that moment, he hardly looked the part of the flamboyant playboy. She tried not to laugh but a little chuckle slipped out. His father was a little tougher than his mother. She sat quietly with the baby while they discussed the issue.

"Mom, I recently found out myself. I didn't know; that's why we're here now." Nigel said in defense of himself. His mother focused her attention on Danielle.

"Danielle, why are we just now learning about the baby?" Danielle felt this was her opportunity to finally be heard. She told part truths to appease her audience.

"Well Mrs. Lancaster, with all due respect. I didn't tell anyone about the pregnancy. My mother died, and Nigel and I weren't getting along. My first thought was I didn't want to be single, unmarried, and raising a child alone. I decided to terminate the pregnancy, but after some soul-searching, I chose to go ahead and keep my baby. I knew Nigel wasn't interested in having children. I didn't want to be a bother to him, so I left him alone and allowed him to live his life."

"Danielle sweetie, I know my son is a philanderer. In fact, he's very whorish and has had his share of women. I know he's not so truthful with them. I've been on him about that since he began dating. I don't like how he treats women, but he's my son, and I love him. One thing I will not stand for; is for one of them to bring a life into this world and not care for that life."

Without going into too much detail, Danielle said, "Ma'am, he really didn't know about our daughter until recently, but now that he knows, he's shown great interest in being a part of her life. He's expressed to me in detail how he's willing to do everything within his ability to ensure she's well taken care of. Why he's even asked me to marry him but we're going to put that on hold for now. We'll be moving in together first; isn't that right Honey?" She cut her eyes at Nigel.

He chuckled nervously. He looked at Danielle, then back at his mother. "Yeah, that's right."

His mother said, "Well that sounds great, although it's difficult for me to believe that Nigel asked you to marry him. You must be a very special young lady. I didn't think any woman had it in her to turn this one around. He's a mess child. Are you sure that this is what you want, or better yet, are you truly in love?" She looked into his eyes to see if he would be honest with her.

He looked away and said, "Mom, it's what I want."

"Are you doing this for the baby Nigel?"

"Partly; but I think Danielle and I can make it work."

"You need to be sure because a woman's heart is nothing to play with; neither is a child. I know many people who co-parent without being married or living together. Some people stay together for the sake of the child, but they soon end up resenting one another. That's why I'm asking."

Nigel walked over to his mother and kissed her on the cheek. "Mom, I'm a man; I know what I want. I've been playing the field for a while. It's time that I settle down. At least allow us the chance to try, before you go shooting it down." Although Mrs. Lancaster wasn't convinced that the move was a good one, she conceded.

"Alright son, but remember what I said."

"I will, Mom."

They continued playing with the baby and conversing. As they were doing so, Chad came in. Nigel was uncomfortable. He wasn't prepared to see Chad. Still grieving and in a somber mood, Chad briefly scanned the room. His mother looked up at him with concern seeing his worn expression.

"Hey son, how are you feeling this afternoon?"

"I'm a better mother." Chad noticed Danielle and Nigel. He saw the baby in her arms.

"Chad, meet Danielle," his mother said.

"Hello Danielle."

Chad was puzzled because he knew Danielle was the very woman who had set Nigel's home on fire and had been harassing him. He wondered why she would be visiting his parents and standing in their living room. He asked, "What's going on here?"

"Well Chad, this here is your niece, Miracle Denise," his mother said. He could barely speak.

"My...my niece?" Chad looked at the baby. He, too, noticed the resemblance to his mother. Thinking about Blaire and his own child, he teared up. He stared at the baby for a minute. He was a bit jealous. He wished she were his daughter. He was hurt. He felt the universe dealt him a cruel blow. He was the good guy, but his fiancé and baby died while his brother, the bad guy, got the baby and the girl. He wanted to be happy for Nigel, but he couldn't, at least not now. Not only was he not happy, but he was also alarmed that Danielle was in his parent's home knowing what she was capable of.

He called his brother's name, "Nigel, let me speak with you for a moment." They walked out back on the patio. They walked down towards the lake where they couldn't be disturbed. Chad got in his face,

"What in the hell do you think you are doing man?"

"What do you mean?"

"Man, you brought that damn girl to our parent's home. Now she knows where they live. It's not enough that she sets your house on fire, which makes her a criminal; now she knows how to come here. If she starts anything with Mom and Dad, I'm not playing Nigel; you both will have to answer to me."

"Trust me man, I have her under control."

"If that were true, she wouldn't have had you on the run; and what's up with this baby?" Chad asked.

"Look man, that's why she's here. I just found out about the baby. That's why she was so upset. She was pregnant when I broke it off with her and she went on this rampage. I treated her poorly I admit that, but had I known about the baby, I wouldn't have been such a jerk. She only told me recently. I talked with her and we're trying to work something out."

"It's obvious you believe she's your daughter"

"Man, did you see that baby?"

"Yes, I saw her. She looks just like Mom, but still, I think you need to get a paternity test before you allow this crazy female back into your life. Women these days are just as bad as men, especially when they know a man has money. You need to get a paternity test for sure and get her crazy ass out of my momma's house."

"I'll get the test done man, but I want to tell you, she and the baby will be moving in with me." Chad looked at him and said,

"Really dude? Are you serious? I see you still haven't learned. I would be afraid to even sleep in the same house with her. You may not wake up. But it'll serve you right. You're so damn hard-headed. You only want what you want. How long do you plan on playing daddy and husband? You said yourself your dick would get bored with just one woman."

"Man, you're just like Mom, always worried about me. I'll be alright."

"Remember, Nigel, It's not just Danielle in this picture; that baby doesn't need any of your drama. Kids need more than a playboy for a father, especially little girls." Chad briefly lost his composure thinking of Blaire and his unborn child.

"What's wrong man?" Nigel knew but he asked anyway.

"I found out recently that Blaire was pregnant. I was going to be a father too. Nigel placed his hand on Chad's shoulder.

"Man, I'm sorry to hear about that." Chad moved away from his brother. He didn't want to be comforted.

Nigel said, "I love you man."

"I'm sorry Nigel man; it's not you. I mean, I should be happy for you, but it's so hard. Look, I'm going through a lot emotionally right now; please don't take it personally."

"You're good man, I understand." Nigel patted him on the back, and he went back into the house to where his mother and Danielle were.

A few minutes later, Chad went inside. He mingled with everyone, making small talk, mostly talking with his parents while keeping a watchful eye on Danielle and his brother. He looked at the baby. She smiled at him which warmed his heart. Her smile briefly made him forget about his pain. He talked to her in baby talk. He reached for her, and she went to him. He played with her for a few minutes then he gave her back to her mother when his phone rang. It was Jessica.

"Hello"

"Hey Chad, can you come over here now? I want to speak with you."

"What is it, Jessica?"

"I'll let you know when you get here." Nigel overheard him saying Jessica's name. He became alarmed.

"Was that Jessie?" He asked.

"Yeah man."

"Well, what did she want?"

"She didn't say, she wants me there now. She'll tell me when I get there."

"I want to go with you."

"I got this. You need to stay here and tend to your business," he said looking over at Danielle and the baby. Nigel really wanted to know what Jessica had to tell Chad. He looked at Danielle and asked,

"Danielle, do you mind staying here for a while so I can ride with my brother?" She looked baffled. Before she could give him an answer, his father said,

"Nigel, you need to stay here with your family. It's impolite of you to bring her here and leave her around someone she barely knows. Chad will be okay."

Chad hurried out the door. Nigel began to worry even more. He tried calming his mind. He continued with the visit for a few more minutes. He made up an excuse to leave. He and Danielle got the baby and said goodbye to his parents and left. On the ride back to his place, he asked,

"You didn't say anything to anybody did you?" She looked at him, almost confused, and said, "No, I haven't; you've given me no reason to, have you? I'm not trying to destroy you, Nigel, well at least not at the moment. I want what's rightfully owed to me and Miracle. I wouldn't play my hand that soon, it wouldn't serve any purpose. Besides, I still have some feelings left in my heart for you. I don't hate you entirely. Because of you, I have my beautiful daughter."

"Well, our friend Jessica is a private detective and she's helping with the case. She just called Chad with some important news. I want to know what's happening, so I'll drop you and the baby off at my place, and I'll see you when I'm done, okay." She agreed to go to his place. Nigel dropped them off and called Chad. He got no answer, so he rushed over to the detective agency. When he got there, Mrs. Barnes was there but Jessica was gone. He asked about her whereabouts, but she didn't say.

Jessica decided to meet Chad at the local sandwich shop downtown. It was a normal hangout for the police, who loved to meet up for a quick bite. Jessica, a former police officer, still loved the place. She was waiting when he arrived. He took a seat and placed his order. Jessica didn't want to come right out and say she may have suspected his brother, so she eased into the conversation with a little small talk.

"So, Jessica, what do you want to talk to me about?" Trying not to look too concerned, she said, "It's nothing, really. I just wanted to make sure you were holding up okay. I do have a couple of questions for you, though."

"Okay, go ahead."

"How are you doing?"

"I'm making it, but I won't be able to rest until this son of a bitch is caught."

"So how are Mr. and Mrs. Lancaster doing?"

"They're fine."

"I'm sure they're being a great support system for you. How about Nigel? How's he doing?"

"You know Nigel. It is, what it is with him. He has always been self-centered, but I have to admit he's been supportive of me during this time. That's something I'd never come to expect from him. I guess everyone has some good in them. He seems to be turning over a new leaf too. Remember that girl that set his house on fire?"

"Talking about the stalker? Mom told me about that. Did the police ever find her?"

"No, but apparently Nigel did. It turns out that she has a baby, and she says Nigel is the father. She's never told anyone about the child until now. Now we both know Nigel is a womanizer and he beds many women. He finally met his match with this one. She's introduced him to the baby and now he wants to be a part of the child's life. He says he's going to be a father to the baby and they're moving in together."

Jessica's jaw dropped. "What? Did you say that Nigel is talking about settling down and becoming a daddy? I find that hard to believe."

"Perhaps this baby has changed his mind. Maybe all that's happened with Blaire has caused something in him to take a closer look at his own life. I don't know. You can never tell what's going to happen from day to day with him. I try not to get too involved with his personal business. As long as the company is running okay and my investments are secure, and if he keeps Mom and Dad out of it, I couldn't care less who the hell he's having sex with. He brought her and the baby by to meet Mom and Dad. I was surprised at that. I told him if that woman does anything to upset my parents, they both will have to answer to me."

"Are you serious? He brought them over?"

"Yes, and the baby looks just like our family, she is so beautiful, and she has a strong resemblance to Mom. I mean she looks just like her. I told him to get a paternity test anyway. He said he would."

By now, the wheels were turning in Jessica's head, and her detective instincts were beginning to kick in. She shifted the subject to the area she wanted from the beginning. "Oh okay, how often did you see Nigel in Miami?"

"Almost daily."

"Where was he at the time Blaire died, do you know?"

"No, I wouldn't know that. There's no telling about Nigel. He had found so many women in Miami, that I thought he had gotten lost out there."

"Was he in Miami?"

"To tell you the truth Jessie, I have no clue where he was. I was working hard on trying to wrap up work on the Kensington's yacht. I spoke with him earlier in the day and I assumed he was in Miami. He never said anything different, but you can never tell about Nigel."

"Do you think he could've been in Arkansas during that time?" Chad looked at Jessica concerned.

"Wait a minute; are you trying to say Nigel may have had something to do with Blaire's death?"

"I'm just trying to see where everyone was during that time."

"Jessie sweetie, you're barking up the wrong tree. Now I know you were on the force, and you solved many homicides. It's a known fact that you're an amazing detective, but please believe me when I tell you that my brother is not capable of hurting anyone in that way. Yeah, I know he's a womanizer, but he would never physically hurt a woman least of all Blaire. Now if you're steering your investigation into that arena, you need to find another mark. To tell you the truth, I don't like what you're insinuating."

"Chad, you came to me and asked me to help you. That's what I'm trying to do. I'm trying to get to the bottom of this. To do so I have to ask the difficult questions."

"I'm beginning to regret I even came to you. Instead of everyone going after the real killer, everyone seems to be going after me or my family." She slipped in another question while he was yet on the defensive.

"Does Nigel have keys to your place?"

"Of course, he does."

"Chad, there was no sign of forced entry, and why would she freely open the door for someone with whom she's unfamiliar? Now, I would love to eliminate him as a suspect if he's willing to go down and talk to the police and submit a DNA sample, and we can move on to other avenues."

"Look Jessie, I'm not going to sit here and allow you to accuse my brother."

"I'm not accusing Nigel. You know I care about you both. You guys are practically like family to me. I simply want him to submit to a test eliminating him."

Chad was far beyond heated. "Jessie, I can't do this today. I have to go." He stormed out of the restaurant. He didn't wait for his food.

The server came up to her and asked, "Did he leave?"

"Yes, just put it on my bill. I'll need a to-go box please." Jessica exhaled and thought more on the subject. She wasn't convinced Nigel was innocent. The police had no probable cause to ask for his DNA, so if he didn't willingly submit to testing, they would have to have something concrete on him to obtain it.

CHAPTER SIX

Nigel was busy putting up the new crib he had purchased for his daughter. He was no good at it. He was sitting on the floor with pieces everywhere. Chad stopped by to visit as usual. He walked into the bedroom and noticed Nigel sitting on the floor looking frustrated. Nigel looked up at him and said, "Man, it looked so simple at first, but look at all these parts. Screw A into B, and take C, and put it in number one. These damn instructions don't make sense." Chad motioned for him to move over.

"How hard can it be, it's only a crib?"

"Man, I've been working on this thing for hours." Chad got the instruction sheet and looked at it for a minute.

"I see your problem right here. Man, you're doing it all wrong. You weren't reading the instructions right." Chad began putting the crib together as Nigel looked on.

"Man, you were always good with your hands. I could never seem to do things like this. Whenever we needed something put together you would always do it for us. You make it look so easy."

"You were too impatient to do things like this. All it takes is a little time and patience."

"I can't seem to do anything right. Hell, I can't even put a crib together for my own daughter." Chad looked at Nigel seeing his frustration. Feeling a little sorry for him he asked,

"So, you're really going through with this huh?"

"Yes, it seems as though I am."

"Nigel this is not just about you anymore but that baby. Babies need time and patience, and they don't come with an instruction booklet. You must be fully committed because a child's well-being is at stake. She's not like all the women you've been with. You can't be all excited and ready to play daddy today and then dispose of her tomorrow. If you're not fully committed to this, you don't need to do it. I think you're moving a little too fast if you ask me but it's your life. It's alright to make provisions and all, but you went from calling the police and running from this woman to moving her and her baby in with you. You haven't gotten a paternity test to determine if you're the biological father. You just took some psychotic person's word for it and now you've moved her in."

Nigel looked as if he didn't care about what he was saying. "Look man, I've fucked up so much in my life. I'm not like you. That thing that you were born with that makes you a good man, I wasn't born with it. I've made many mistakes."

Nigel began to feel sad. He wanted to confess to Chad about Blaire, but he knew he couldn't. The guilt was eating away at him. Normally, he could share anything with his brother, but this one thing he couldn't share. He almost sobbed.

"Man, we all make mistakes, and sometimes we make poor choices. You'll get it right one day. If this is your attempt to change your life, I commend you for it, but I'm not sure that this is the right move for you."

"Chad I just want to make things right with my daughter. I want to be in her life and love and protect her. I want her to know her father. If it takes me and Danielle to work out our differences to make that happen then I'll do just that." Nigel wanted to be close to his daughter but his real intentions in moving Danielle in were to keep her quiet. Either way, it served his purpose. Danielle was getting what she wanted and so was he. The brothers worked on the crib together.

"Alright, man, hand me that piece right there. Then all we have to do is tighten these screws, and it'll be finished." Nigel watched as Chad tightened the last two screws.

"Voila! Now my niece will have a nice sturdy crib to sleep in. I'm so glad her daddy didn't put it together." He looked at Nigel and laughed.

"Man, you did that so fast, and you made it look so easy. Why couldn't I have been born with that gift?"

"You have many talents you just don't use them often."

Nigel, feeling undeserving of his brother's love, found it difficult to look him directly in the eye. He had made a devasting mistake, and he wished he could make it right. He knew he could do nothing at this point. He just whispered under his breath, "Chad, I love you. I want to thank you for always believing in me and taking up my causes."

"Hey man, no problem. Putting this bed together with you made me realize that I could've been putting it together for my own daughter. I didn't want to see it negatively. I guess it helped me a little, too, by doing this for my niece."

Nigel's guilty conscience was excruciating.

"Man, I don't deserve you for a brother. You are truly a good man. Whenever I'm in trouble, you're always here for me. When you needed me the most, I let you down." Nigel backed against the wall. "I let you down, man." He wanted to say it. He was almost hysterical.

"Man, you didn't let me down. What are you talking about?" He regained his composure and said,

"It's unfair how many times you've been here for me, and I've never been able to return the favor. You've always bailed me out of all kinds of crap. I'm just a total fuck-up!" Wanting to lighten the mood from the stress and tension his brother was feeling Chad said,

"Yeah, but you are my brother even if you are a fuck-up. Now, why are you getting so deep on me? Where's my little brother? Come on out of there. I come here hoping you would cheer me up and you're over here falling apart."

He hugged his brother. He gave him a loving pat on the back. Poking fun at him he said, "Come on daddy Nigel! Let's go and get a drink and play a game of pool. I know you need a break since you worked so hard at putting this crib together." Chad laughed and Nigel gave a halfhearted smile. Feeling undeserving of the kindness being shown to him, he thought, *"He's so good to me. He's comforting me because I'm feeling guilty for killing his fiancé and his unborn child. I don't deserve his love. I wish I could take it all back. I'm going to make this up to him one day if it's the last thing I do."* Chad helped him clean up the mess and they left.

They made it to the bar and Nigel set the pool table while Chad ordered their drinks. They began to play a few games. Chad was waiting his turn. Looking at his brother, he was a little proud of him for what he believed was the possible beginning of him turning over a new leaf.

"You know Nigel, I'm kind of proud of you for standing up and doing what you feel is the right thing with the baby. I apologize for being so hard on you recently."

"Nah, it's cool, I understand. I haven't exactly been a choir boy in life. I know everyone knows I'm a bit selfish at times." Chad cleared his throat very loudly and laughed. "Okay yeah, I'm selfish. I can admit to that, but I don't think of it so much as being selfish. I see things in life, and I go after them. If I don't get it, somebody else will so I figure it might as well be me. I'm beginning to see the many negative effects of my behavior on others. I've done many things to people which I now regret. I've done things to women, business associates, and even my own family that I'm not proud of." He looked at Chad.

"Chad, man I'm sorry to you for all the pain I've caused. I've been a rotten brother man. I don't deserve you. Not only are you my brother, but you're my friend and the only real advocate I've had in my life. I mean when we became adults, you could've easily gone your own way, but you continued to look after me. You made sure I had just as much as you; even after I fucked up that business deal, you never turned your back on me. I want you to know no matter what happens to me in the future, I truly do love you. I want you to remember that."

"Thanks, man, you are turning over a new leaf. I'm amazed at you. I've never heard anything like this coming from you. Normally you're so harsh and brash and loud. Who are you and what have you done with my little brother?"

"No, man I'm just reflecting on my past. You know I liked Danielle before all this happened with her. If I was ever going to settle down, she made me feel as if she would be the one."

"So why did you decide against it?"

"To be honest, I was afraid of the way she made me feel. I knew I was falling for her, so I began to sabotage it. It was never her fault. I treated her poorly and I said some of the meanest things to her man. Another reason was, that although I liked her, I still wanted to play around. I wanted her and my other women too. Why can't I seem to control my sexual urge for women? I mean how do you do it, bro? You seem to have your life under control. I have to have sex daily. You can go about your life without even thinking about it."

Chad said, "I keep myself focused on work. I love what I do. Hey, I have a high sex drive as with any red-blooded American male. Rather than having sex with some random female, I just focus on things that matter to me. I could live my life like you, carefree, full of sex and partying, but where would that get me? It's all about balance and having your life prioritized. If you base your life around sex, you'll soon find yourself lacking. You must find what you're passionate about and pursue it. I have many things I'm passionate about. To tell you the truth, before I met my Blaire, I had one young lady I would often see on the days, I only wanted female company. She and I had a mutual understanding. We longed for the warm touch and the heated passion of a sexual liaison. We both knew we were too busy for a relationship. We helped each other on many nights. We kept it real with one another and we did our thing. That's why I said if you're honest with a lady about what you want, there should be no backlash. Besides, in this day and time, you can't be too careful. There are all sorts of diseases floating around. Sleeping with multiple partners could prove to be deadly. These women nowadays are willing to do just about anything to get or trap a man, especially if they see a potential payday from it. A lot of brothers play into the men's shortage game, and they play around, not thinking of the consequences of their actions. Some women are very possessive, so you must know who you're dealing with. If you pick the wrong one, it could change your life forever."

After listening to Chad, Nigel said, "I was just thinking if some guy treats my little Miracle like trash, I will kill him, yet I have done it not only to Danielle but to countless other women. Having a baby daughter makes you reflect on your own bullshit. I've fucked up in life; I hope my daughter doesn't have to bear the sins of my past on her shoulders."

"She won't have to man. Just bring her up properly and she will be a perfect young lady. I can see Mom and Dad are already in love with her. I must admit, she steals your heart. I like the thought of being an uncle. I was sad learning about my child but seeing Miracle has helped me see the future and not the past. I want to see Blaire's killer brought to justice and yes, I'm obsessed with finding her killer, but I hated the man I was becoming. I was angry all the time and full of bitterness. I'm still hurting, and I feel cheated. I wanted Blaire, but lately, it's like she's been sending me little signs of her love. I've stopped obsessing and now I'm starting to feel her love. I feel she doesn't want me obsessing but she wants me to remember the good times we shared. That's what I'm going to focus on. It seems the police are nowhere near solving her murder anyway and they're focusing on all the wrong people. Even Jessie is focusing on the wrong person. Do you know what she said to me when I went by there the other day? She was hinting at the thought that perhaps you may have had something to do with her death."

Nigel laughed nervously. "What would make her think that?"

"She asked me if you were in Little Rock when Blaire was killed. Can you imagine she would point fingers at my brother? I told her if you were here, it had nothing to do with Blaire. She wants you to submit a DNA sample so they can rule you out as a suspect. I couldn't hear any more of her foolish talk, so I left. I wish they would focus more on the real killer and stop focusing on my family. I understand they must rule everybody out who is close to her but why they would go after my brother is beyond me. I guess next they will investigate Dad too."

"That's a damn shame," Nigel said shaking his head. They continued talking but now Nigel was more on edge than ever from learning what was said by his brother. They played a few more games of pool and left. Nigel called Danielle. He asked her to come over. She hadn't moved in yet. She did bring a few of her and the baby's things to the home. She came over and they ordered dinner. He played with the baby and after she was asleep, he sat Danielle down and talked with her. He looked at her sincerely.

"Danielle, I want to talk to you for a minute." She looked at him earnestly wondering what he was about to say. "I have some things I want to say to you. It's been eating me up inside, and I have no one else I can tell but you." She looked at him curiously as he continued speaking.

"I lied to you when I told you I was only using you for sex. I was a coward hiding behind my true feelings. The truth is I was falling in love with you, but I didn't want to change my ways. I wanted you, but I wanted to keep playing around too, and I know I couldn't do that and be in a serious relationship. I knew you would never stand for that, so I left you. Facing you would force me to have to admit my feelings for you. That was something I wanted to keep hidden. I must tell you; I actually missed you when we weren't together. When you showed up here that day, I wanted to hurt you, so I said some hurtful things to make you go away. After the fire, I was angry and confused. I felt you didn't want me anymore and it seemed you were hell-bent on destroying me, so I knew I had to move away for a while. That's when I went to Miami. When I got there, I met Blaire Kensington through my brother. I was curious about her. She and my brother were not dating at the time. I have to admit I wanted her.

The more I saw her, the more I wanted her. I don't know what happened to me. Something just took over me. I was overwhelmed with feelings of attraction for her. I couldn't stay away.

When she and my brother began dating, I didn't think it was serious and thought I could make her choose me. I don't know what was going on inside my head, but I couldn't get rid of the aching feeling for her. It taunted me day and night. I followed her around town hoping she would notice me. She did, but when she realized it was me and not Chad, she wouldn't bite.

While she was in Arkansas, knowing my brother was in Miami, I came here to talk to her. I wanted to persuade her to give me a chance. When I walked in, she was lying in bed. I watched her for a while as she slept, as I had done many times before. I longed for her to be mine. I sat next to her and kissed her. She opened her eyes and kissed me back. I was shocked. I was going to tell her who I was, but my need to make love to her overtook me, and I allowed her to believe I was my brother. I used this chance to my advantage, thinking perhaps it would further my cause of gaining her affection. I knew I shouldn't have crossed the line, but I couldn't help myself. I had been yearning for it from the moment I met her. My mind said no, but everything in me said yes. I knew this would be my only chance, and it would have to be the performance of a lifetime. When she found out I had tricked her, instead of stopping there, I continued to try to convince her. While making love to her, she began to cry.

"It was an accident. I had no intention of hurting her. You have to believe me, Danielle. I didn't go there to kill her." Danielle could see the sorrow and regret in him. She pulled him close to her and said,

"I'm sure you didn't mean to do it. But why would you want to destroy your brother's happiness?"

"I wasn't thinking about that; I was caught up in the moment. After that, I just...I don't know."

Danielle said, "We all make mistakes, and I must admit you've made some huge ones. Initially, I fell in love with you because I saw some good in you. You showed me a side of you that was kind, generous, and loving. Then you changed on me. You were just as cruel as you were kind. I wanted to make you pay, so I responded negatively. After I found out I was pregnant, I lost it emotionally. I wanted to kill you. I can understand how our emotions can get the best of us. But Blaire was innocent. What is it about you that loves to destroy innocent people?"

"I told you, Danielle, I didn't do it on purpose. It was an accident." She sat back on the sofa and looked at him. She wasn't sure what to think.

"So why are you opening up to me?"

"Shit, I don't know, maybe because out of all the people I know, you're the one who I think is most genuine, and besides, who else can I go to and tell this secret? I need somebody to talk to, and since you already know, I may as well explain what happened."

"Remember, I witnessed most of it, so it'll take a minute for me to process what you've shared with me. What I want to know is, are you using me now since you say you're being honest? I know I have a lot on you, but are you using this as an opportunity to keep me quiet, or do you genuinely want to have a relationship with me and your daughter?"

"Danielle, I've told many lies in my past, and I've hurt so many people. I have nothing else to hide, and it's a relief to be able to get things off my chest. Trust me, the sole reason I have you here is our daughter. Another reason is, as I told you, I fell for you. And last, yes, I wanted to keep you quiet, but that doesn't take precedence over our daughter. The truth is, Danielle, I like you with your crazy ass. I guess out of desperation, you did what you felt you had to do, considering I gave you no choice. Me having broken things off while you were pregnant. I can see how you were hurt. I hear that women's hormones are off the chart while they're pregnant. I shouldn't have been such an asshole, but you should've told me back then you were pregnant. I know that would've made a big difference. I hate I missed the pregnancy and the entire experience of being a first-time father. It took all of this for you to get my attention. I truly apologize."

Danielle continued to listen. "I was with my brother today, and he said that our family friend Jessie, the private detective, thinks I was in town. It seems she suspects me, and she wants me to go to the police for a DNA test to eliminate me as a suspect. I can tell you that's not going to happen, and the only way they get me in there is if they have a warrant because I won't go willingly. If my parents or my brother find out the truth, it would devastate them, and I'll do whatever I need to keep it quiet. I just don't know how long I'll be able to do so."

"So, what are you going to do?"

"I'm not sure right now, but I want to spend as much time as I can with you and Miracle."

Danielle liked the sound of that. She was still in love with Nigel. She began to let down her guard. She believed him, and he confided in her as he used to. He appeared to be a different man, like he was seeing things from a new perspective. He pulled her close to him, and she laid her head on his chest. He played with her hair. They lay there together, rekindling their former friendship through light stories and innocent play until Miracle woke from her nap.

Danielle sprang from the sofa to get her. Nigel said,

"Relax, I got her." She hesitated for a moment. Nigel went in to get the baby. She was standing inside the crib, holding on to the bars, looking for her mother. Since she wasn't in her usual bed, she was afraid. Nigel lifted her from her crib and began rocking her. He sang to her and talked to her in baby language. Danielle had come with a sippy cup and pamper to change her. She didn't disturb him. She stood back and watched as he continued to play with her. She looked on and smiled. He seemed as if he were a happy father. He turned around and saw Danielle.

"She stopped crying when I picked her up and sang to her. I think she is starting to like me. Do you think she knows I'm her daddy?" Danielle smiled and said,

"I'm almost sure of it." He helped to change her diaper.

Nigel said, "I want to protect her. I want to protect you both. I don't know what's going to happen to me in the near future, but I want to make sure she's well taken care of."

She smiled and said, "That's all I ever wanted."

Danielle was content with the fact that Nigel had begun to recognize his mistake and owned up to it. She had been so in love with him that she put aside the very fact that he had abandoned her and was now a murderer. In the sickest and twisted of ways, she reasoned within that as long as he was willing to acknowledge her and take care of his child, she was prepared to forgive him and keep his secret! She would never give him up to the police. In her mind, she has gotten what she always wanted, and she will allow nothing to destroy it, even if it means protecting a rapist and killer. Two unhealthy individuals feeding off the desperations of one another could only prove disastrous for all involved, with an innocent child caught in the middle.

CHAPTER SEVEN

Jessica was determined to get to the bottom of the case for Chad. The police department was still investigating, but they weren't aggressively investigating Nigel. Although she had her suspicions about Nigel's guilt, and so did Detective Armstrong, she wasn't prepared to admit it to anyone. She grew up with Nigel and Chad. Since she was close to the family, she wanted to be sure she was right before outright accusing him. She hopped on her crotch rocket and rode over to one of her dad's favorite spots. It was Willow Beach Park on the north side of the city by the Arkansas River. Her father would take her fishing there. She liked to go there and reflect.

She rode through the park and pulled her bike up to the picnic table. She took her helmet off and sat on the table overlooking the river. This is where her parents would set up the barbecue grills and fish on the river when they weren't on the boat. Several times a year, the Barnes and the Lancaster family would enjoy days by the river or on the pontoon boat and have a family day. She smiled as she reminisced about the wonderful times they all shared. Nigel would chase her around the park, trying to kiss her. Her dad would warn her about him. As they got older, her father would hint at her possibly dating Chad and although he took her to their prom, she had no romantic feelings for him whatsoever. He felt more like family to her, and she wasn't interested in dating him.

Nigel was always on the prowl. She had to basically watch him at every turn, especially when they were in their late teens. Nigel's dad would brag about him being a lady's man at such a young age, and when Jessica's father noticed he had eyes for her, he immediately went to work on his daughter, warning her against him. Nigel was tolerated more than anything, and his presence tended to annoy her. He was egotistical and arrogant and tended to be a bit pushy, all of which she hated about him.

The twins looked identical, but knowing them personally, she could easily tell them apart by their disposition. That's why she began to wonder about the relationship between Nigel and Blaire, and she wanted to know more about it. If the lady was beautiful, as in Blaire's case, she was almost sure he was his same old pushy, obnoxious self. She began to devise a plan to flush out the real killer, but she needed Chad on her side, and at this point, he was unwilling to speak with her about the matter. Especially if she would be accusing his brother.

In the meantime, Chad flew to Miami to spend time with Blaire's parents. The media was still covering the news of her death. He was bombarded with media coverage. He gave a few interviews, stating his feelings about the case, and continued to express his desire to find the killer. He continued to ask for privacy and asked for mercy and prayer during their time of sorrow. Most of them understood, while others still wanted an exclusive story. He went to the family estate and was warmly greeted by both her parents. His presence seemed to ease their pain. They knew how much he and Blaire adored each other. The thought of him having something to do with her death never crossed their mind, even though the police informed them that there was a strong possibility that he may have been involved.

Chad looked at the large portrait of her hanging over the mantle. He was drawn to it. He went over and stared at it as if he could bring her back by looking at it. Emotions flooded his soul as he looked at her beautiful face, thinking of all the times they kissed. He thought of her smile and the way her nose wrinkled when she laughed. He wanted to stroke her hair. He longed for her soft touch. If only he could hear her voice calling his name once again. Her parents allowed him a few minutes to reflect without saying a word. They both walked over to where he was standing.

Mrs. Kensington slipped her hand into his, giving it a tight squeeze. He turned and hugged her.

"I miss her so much," he said. Mr. Kensington walked up to him and said,

"So do we, son."

He pulled himself together. "I apologize for my display of emotion. I came by to check on you. I just wanted to spend a little time with you. It makes me feel better to be around someone who loved her too."

They continued comforting each other while speaking of Blaire and their wonderful times. They discussed the investigation. The night went well, and Chad went to his condo after the visit. He looked around the place. He saw signs of Blaire everywhere. He decided to lie across his bed with the lights dimmed while overlooking the ocean and thinking about his love. As he looked in the farthest distance, he could see her smiling at him. He was comforted by his thoughts and fell asleep.

Jessica was busy investigating Danielle. She rode by Nigel's place and saw her vehicle in the driveway. She called Detective Armstrong and asked him to do a little research on her. Indeed, the police had been looking for her for the arson and the vandalism of Nigel's property, and there was an active warrant for her arrest. Although they had no probable cause to bring Nigel in, bringing her in would prove to be rather interesting. The police staked out the home, waiting for Danielle to come out. They spotted her as she and Nigel were on their way to purchase more things for the baby's room. Their vehicle was blocked, and officers immediately took her into custody. "Danielle Turner, we have an outstanding warrant for your arrest for arson and felony vandalism." Nigel was visibly shaken as he initially thought they were coming for him. After they told Danielle why she was being arrested, she willingly went with them, but Nigel demanded her release. He was asked not to interfere but invited to come to the station to bail her out.

She was taken to the station for booking, but Nigel was there immediately to bail her out. He tried to convince them that they had the wrong person, and he wanted the charges dropped against her. He told them he had made a mistake and that it was someone else. They knew he was lying to protect her. They proceeded to book her in. Her medium-length hair covered her silky, light-brown face as she held her head down while she was being escorted away. With her hands cuffed in front of her, she swiped at her hair, removing it from her face as her photo was taken. After that, she was fingerprinted. After officially being booked in, she was taken to an interrogation room where she was questioned about the arson. She looked at the female detective as she was speaking with her about the criminal charges. Her youthful eyes welled with tears as she thought of her daughter being without her. A middle-aged white female investigator who had been assigned to the case walked into the room and said, "Ms. Turner, my name is Detective Joycelyn Hill. I've been investigating this case for a while now. You've been charged with arson, which in this case is a class Y felony punishable by up to ten to forty years in the federal correctional facility. Also, you've been charged with second-degree criminal mischief. Care to tell me what happened here?" Danielle was very respectful, but when the detective questioned her, she politely declined to speak with her, exercising her right to remain silent until speaking with her attorney. Detective Hill immediately stopped the interview. Danielle was allowed to make her phone call, which she used to call Nigel, who was still out waiting in the front of the jail with the baby. From the other room, Jessica had been allowed to watch Danielle's brief encounter with the detective while she was being questioned through the one-way window. Nigel never noticed Jessica, and she planned it that way. In the meantime, Danielle was placed in a holding cell until she could see the judge and make bail. The following day, Danielle was released after Nigel posted bail for her. The charges couldn't be dropped due to direct evidence that linked her to the arson. The state picked up the charges, so whether Nigel wanted to proceed or not didn't matter.

Nigel was waiting for her with the baby as she was released. She grabbed her baby and held her close to her breast. Nigel kissed her on the cheek.

"Are you okay Danielle?" She was a little agitated by the question, and she felt it was partly his fault for not dropping the charges against her.

"No, I'm not okay. That was a horrible experience." They took my fingerprints, and now I have a mugshot like a common criminal. My mother is probably rolling over in her grave."

"I'm sorry Danielle, I tried to drop the charges against you, but they told me I couldn't. It was out of my hands."

They quickly walked to the car. He reached for the baby so he could put her in the car seat. "I'll do it myself," she snapped. She struggled to put the baby in the car seat. The baby became fussy. Nigel gently pulled Danielle out of the way. He picked up the baby and gently rocked her in his arms. He spoke calmly to her, and she stopped fussing. With the baby secure in one arm, he took his free hand, took Danielle by the arm, and gently pulled her close to him. He calmed her. "Come here baby."

He held her. He kissed her. She was comforted. "I'm sorry baby. I know you were afraid. It's my fault. I should've been a better man. It was my stupidity that got you in this predicament. Trust me, I'm going to do everything I can to make this all go away. You won't be convicted of this crime. I hired the best attorney money can buy." After he was sure she was at ease, he said, "Now, let's go and get you something to eat." They left the jail.

Investigators continued to work on Nigel's arson case. Danielle's phone records indicated exactly where she was during the arson as well as on the days before, during, and after her crimes. Also, a doorbell camera from a home in Nigel's neighborhood showed her committing arson. It was also discovered through her phone records that she had been in Arkansas around the area of Chad's place during the estimated time of Blaire's murder. Although there was no sign of female DNA, they began to wonder why she was there and what role, if any, she played in the death of Blaire. Jessica called homicide Detective Byron Armstrong by phone and discussed the case further. Jessica said,

"So Armstrong, this chick stalks Nigel and sets fire to his home. Running from her, he goes to Miami. She ends up in Miami and rents an apartment there. Her cell phone shows her in Arkansas during the time of Blaire's murder. I wonder if she mistook Chad for Nigel and thought that perhaps Blaire was Nigel's lover. Perhaps she could've killed Blaire in a fit of jealousy."

"Yeah, Barnes, but the problem is that there's no evidence of her being inside the home. Remember, this was a violent crime. Besides, her fingerprint didn't match with that on the cell phone."

Jessica said, "You stated that after the murder, she drove back to Miami. Then, when the brothers came to Arkansas, she came back, too. Do you think it's possible she could've been following Nigel?"

"Anything's possible. She's shown up everywhere else he's been."

"I'm willing to bet that she knows something. Maybe she saw something as she was stalking him. If so, she could've been following Nigel to his brother's place the night of the murder. Perhaps she knows what happened that evening. Can you at least look up Nigel's phone records?" Detective Armstrong shook his head and said,

"Not unless we can show probable cause, and that doesn't seem feasible because we don't even have any evidence linking him to the crime; it's only speculation. It appears he was in Miami at the time of her death. The only thing we can hope for is that Nigel will voluntarily give us a sample of his DNA; otherwise, we have no case against him at this time."

"Something strange is going on Armstrong. We need to take a closer look at Nigel because he's been acting pretty suspicious lately. After authorities received a call that she'd vandalized his property again, he later hooked up with his stalker and then moved her into his home. Am I missing something? Doesn't that sound kind of odd to you, Armstrong? Another thing: Nigel came by the agency asking questions about the death of Blaire and how far along we were on the case. He was alarmed when I told him Blaire was pregnant. He seemed nervous and fidgety."

"Well, he was pretty adamant about us dropping the charges against Danielle. Maybe he's just thinking about his child's mother and his baby's care. He could've had a change of heart once he realized he was a father. I know I would've if I were in his shoes. Maybe he feels fortunate to have a daughter of his own, and that's probably why he was upset when you told him Ms. Kensington was pregnant. I don't know. What I do know is that I'm ready to get this case solved. I've got the media hounding me daily, as well as her parents and her fiancé Chad Lancaster. It's all over the airwaves. Podcasters are setting up their own scenarios on who could've killed her. This case has taken over our entire department, and the sooner we solve it, the better it will be for the family, and everyone involved. If we can exclude Nigel, that would be great.

"If he's guilty, he won't volunteer a sample of his DNA or fingerprints, and since we know he's hired a very good attorney for Danielle, I'm sure he won't allow either of them to speak about the case."

"Well, you're pretty close to him, Barnes; perhaps you can convince him to come down and speak with us."

"And what if I can't get him to cooperate?" She asked.

"I'm sure you'll think of something. Barnes, I gotta get this other line; I'll talk to you soon."

Jessica knew getting Nigel to go to the station wasn't going to happen, but she had a plan. She knew exactly how to get the DNA from him. She had to be careful because Nigel was no fool. She had her mother set up a dinner gathering with the family under the guise of a baby shower for the baby. That way, they knew he would show up. It would be held at the Lancaster home.

She went out and purchased gifts for the baby. She also purchased champagne for the couple. She knew Nigel smoked cigars, so she bought the best. What man doesn't deserve a cigar after the birth of his first child, she thought. It was all fitting into her plan. She purchased an expensive bottle of Cognac. It was a pricier brand. At a thousand dollars a bottle, it was sure to impress. It was a perfect gift for Nigel and Mr. Lancaster to share along with a few other male guests. It's expected that the men would drift off and allow the women to talk, especially during an event such as a baby shower. The event was planned for the following Saturday. Jessica was on edge.

She wanted it to be much sooner. She hoped that Nigel was innocent for the sake of the family, but in her heart, she felt he could very well be guilty. As much as she wanted to rule him out, she knew the possibility of his involvement must be considered. If he were indeed innocent, she could focus on helping find the real killer. She hoped her gut instincts were deceiving her, but in her many years in law enforcement, her instincts were usually accurate.

Chad was still in Miami. He decided to throw himself into his work. He and Mr. Kensington got together to discuss putting up a reward for anyone who could aid them in solving the crime. After settling on a reward of five hundred thousand dollars, they called the police and the media. They decided they would use the media to their advantage.

The day of the shower had finally arrived, and it was all about the baby. Nigel and Danielle felt honored that the family received her and the baby with warm, receptive love. Jessica's mother was already there. Everyone doted on little Miracle Denise, and she turned on the charm with her lovely eyes and her infectious, adorable smile. Jessica arrived; her intentions were unknown to anyone there. She gave Nigel a warm, loving hug and congratulated the couple. She presented her gifts to Danielle and Nigel. Included was a small financial gift for the baby. "I also have something for the proud father," she said.

"It's customary to have a cigar when you have a baby, so here you are, Nigel. These are for you." She gave Nigel the cognac and the cigars. He was impressed with the gifts, especially the cigars and the cognac. Admiring the cigars she'd chosen, he was quite familiar with the brand and, given his financial status, found them a bit pricey.

"Girl, how did you manage to get these?" He ran the cigar under his nose. He closed his eyes and inhaled the fragrance of the cigar. He immediately prepared it and bit the cap off with his teeth. Nigel biting the end of the cigar was the perfect opportunity to collect his DNA. Since it was an intimate gathering, there would be plenty of opportunities to do so during the evening. Nigel admired the bottle of Cognac and said,

"You sure picked a fine bottle of cognac. How much did this set you back?"

"Not more than the cigars. I tell ya, I had to take out a small loan for those." Knowing Jessica was loaded with cash, they both laughed.

After chatting with Nigel, the men went to the back of the home near the deck to smoke and drink. Jessica sat with the ladies, making small talk. She made her way to the back for a few minutes and had a drink herself so as not to raise any suspicion from Nigel. She marked where Nigel was sitting and noted where his glass was and the cigar he was smoking. She would come back and forth between chatting with the ladies and sharing a drink with the guys all the while keeping her eyes on Nigel. She talked with Danielle and found her to be a very nice person. She was puzzled as to why she would want to associate with Nigel. She could almost understand why she would commit arson because Nigel was quite the asshole and perhaps deserving of far worse. Unsure of her true motives, she studied her throughout the evening. Was it money or was it love Danielle sought from him? Whatever the reason, Jessica was convinced she held the clue to solving Blaire's case. She was cautious not to ask too many questions or get too invasive. Knowing that Jessica was working the case, Danielle monitored her conversation and tried to talk as little as possible. She answered minimal questions and carefully chose her words. The men were having a wonderful time, and the cognac and great conversations were flowing. Jessica joined in. She hung out with them for a while. The cognac was taking its effect on Nigel, which she'd been waiting for. Feeling secure enough to out-whit Jessica and pretending he was interested in helping her solve the case, he brought the subject up himself.

"So Jessica, is there any news on this little investigation of yours?" She looked at him and thought, *"Well, there he is. Yeah, you sly, smug motherfucker talk to me. Give me the ammo I need to sink your lowdown ass."*

She tried not to get into her feelings as he spoke. She was insulted as he began to try to undermine her intelligence and out-whit her by placing her in the same category as the gullible women he'd taken advantage of his entire life. But he was no match for her. Sure, she'd slipped up earlier in the evening with the cigar bit, but if he thought he was going to go toe to toe with her, he would be in for a rude awakening. She was ready for him. Setting her ego aside, she played along with him. At this point, she almost hoped he would hang himself.

"No, from what I hear, the police have no new leads. The case is basically at a standstill. I spoke with Chad earlier, and he informed me that he and Blaire's father have put up a reward for anyone who has knowledge leading to the arrest and conviction of the killer. There's a five-hundred-thousand-dollar reward. You know that's a lot of money, and that's just for starters. That man has millions of dollars. From what I hear, soon, it'll possibly go up to a million-dollar reward or probably even more. Someone is bound to come forward with all that money being offered. All they want are answers; so far, all the forensic evidence seems to point to your brother."

Nigel wanted to know what Jessica thought, so he asked, "Do you believe Chad killed Blaire?"

"Although some evidence points to the possibility of him being there, it's inconclusive, and the timing is off. So, do you think your brother was capable of committing this crime?"

Nigel, figuring this was a chance to cast any suspicion away from him, puffed his cigar and exhaled. He looked at her with a sinister expression, hoping she would buy what he was about to sell, and said, "Well, if the evidence points to no one other than Chad, perhaps he possibly had something to do with it. Maybe they got into an argument or something, and things got heated, and he lost his head. I mean, it's been known to happen. If there's no other evidence pointing to anyone else, then I hate to say this, but you may have the right person."

She was sickened by his response. She was amazed at how he could say something so evil about his brother. She quickly retorted, "But Chad was in Miami, and that's a proven fact. The time of death doesn't match up with the time he was in Miami."

"Is the time of death exact, or could they be mistaken?"

"I doubt that. The time of death is backed up by strong evidence. This case is going to take some time, but it'll get solved. Another thing that's puzzling me is why Chad would kill her and hire me to find the killer, then put up the reward, too. That doesn't sound like a guilty man to me. Besides, I've heard from a friend close to the investigation that there's one little tidbit that leads to the *real* killer, but I'm sworn to secrecy."

Cutting her eyes at him, she took a sip of her drink and said, "But I'm here to relax and enjoy spending time with friends and family, and I don't want to discuss this case. I've had a difficult week. I simply want to enjoy my evening." The inquisitive expression on his face spoke volumes. She could tell he wanted more, but she refused to give him anything. She wanted him to squirm and beg for more information. She taunted him a bit more simply on the fact he insulted her intelligence. Afterwards, she faked small chatter with him.

"How have you been doing? I see you're a proud papa." Still trying to be slick and wanting to be one step ahead of her, he felt she was buying into his deception by pretending he was all good.

"Yes, I am. Little Miracle is my adorable princess. She's my little star. She's the best part of me."

"Indeed she is," she said. "I'm happy for you. Chad told me you've made quite the turn-around. I see you're finally getting it together."

They continued to talk until Nigel's cup was almost empty. Jessica went to fix herself another drink. She looked at his glass and said, "I'll get us another drink. She picked up his glass and went to the bar where the liquor was. She purposely dropped his glass on the floor while pretending to be tipsy and said,

"Damn, I'm feeling good and mellow. I'm dropping shit. Looks like I'll have to get you another glass." She set the glass aside where she could get it later. She got a fresh glass and fixed him another drink and handed it to him. They continued drinking and smoking cigars until it got late. Nigel snuffed out his cigar. Jessica swiped it without him knowing. When he returned to look for it, he couldn't find it. He lit another one never suspecting a thing. Jessica placed the glass and the cigar in two separate evidence bags that she brought with her. She slipped them into her purse and placed them in her car and went back inside. After spending a little more time with the family, she said goodbye to everyone, kissed her mother, and left. She called Detective Armstrong and told him what she had. He met with her and immediately took the bags.

Jessica was tired. She was emotionally drained. Her body needed attention; the kind that only her much younger lover Marcus Miller could give. It was rare that she called him, but she was desperate. Marcus was in love with Jessica, and he wanted to make their relationship exclusive. She, on the other hand, enjoyed his companionship but was in no position to commit. In years past she had her share of committed relationships. They were problematic for her. She felt the weighted pressure of her former mates suggesting that she leave law enforcement and find a job more suitable for a woman of her stature. She didn't want to be bogged down with demands of her to be in a committed relationship. Jessica was all woman and she did not need to prove herself to guys who felt intimidated by her career and lifestyle. Since she was wealthy, they often suggested that she be more lady-like and support the community, but she heard, "You need to stay in a woman's place." Jessica wasn't that type of woman. She was a biker who enjoyed riding her motorcycles. She loved hunting and fishing. She was a gun collector. She was also an avid racing fan, and she loved the world of motorsport. Her peers often teased her for being one of a few black women loving a seemingly mostly white, male-dominated sport, but she was no traditional woman. Contrary to what people thought, she had a sexy, feminine side to her. She resented the stereotypes others tried to force on her while offering their unsolicited opinions of what they felt she should be doing with her life and career. Meetings in elite social clubs with uppity women never appealed to her. Writing checks to save the world but never actually lifting a finger while going back to their posh lifestyles and feeling good about themselves was a delusional state of mind, in her opinion. Most of these women had no real clue of how the world worked, and she felt that many were detached from reality. It was a suffocating atmosphere, and she tried to avoid that lifestyle at all costs. Sure, she'd given a portion of her wealth to many charities, but she also contributed to society in ways she seemed fit. Solving crimes was in her blood. As much as she loved working in the department, she enjoyed the freedoms the private sector afforded her. Her hands were not tied to bureaucracy or red tape. No Internal Affairs investigations, no chief of police, or male egos to contend with. Her tactics for getting her man, although they may not have been entirely illegal, sometimes fell within the grey areas of the law and often caused problems for her at the department. But doing so almost always resulted in her solving her cases. So it was with the evidence she'd recently obtained on Nigel by swiping his cigar and his glass to hand over to Detective Armstrong. The chain of evidence may not be admissible, but at least she would know for sure whether he was involved. To her, the only thing that mattered was the truth; even if she knew a conviction may not come of it, at least a killer would be exposed. Little things like that are why she loved working for herself.

As far as relationships were concerned, there were times she considered a serious, more permanent union, but if so, she figured her mate would have to be an older version of Marcus Miller. Marcus was almost fourteen years younger than her. She made it known that although she enjoyed what they shared, she had no interest in a long-term commitment. She felt he would be throwing away his chances to have a much younger mate who could share in his dreams and possibly have a family. She wasn't interested in having children but to a young guy like Marcus who was ready to settle down, she felt he should keep his options open. In addition to wanting him to keep his options open, she felt that as she aged, perhaps he wouldn't find her as appealing later in life. If she allowed the love affair to continue by adding emotions, she could end up suffering the consequences if it failed. So, she tried diligently to subdue her feelings for her protection.

Marcus, however, wasn't deterred by her suggestion. It was Jessica he wanted and as long as she would have him, he was satisfied. Although she said she didn't want him getting too close, he was committed to her and her alone. There was no other woman for him. He was obsessed with her from the moment they met. Her youthful beauty was unlike any woman he'd ever met. Her shapely, well-toned body blew his mind. Her fun, vivacious spirit appealed to him. She could be sophisticated and glamorous in one minute, and she possessed the ability to let down her hair, hop on her bike, and ride it like a professional racer. They shared a love of the great outdoors, traveling, and sports. She had her life together. Although she was very wealthy, she was humble. She was also tough and could handle herself in any situation. Once she allowed him into her space, he knew he would do anything to remain in her life. Nothing was worth losing her, and he's proved his love and loyalty to her ever since. It was true that he was ready to settle down, and it was Jessica he wanted to have for the rest of his life.

Jessica called him. "Hi Jessica, he said." She could hear in his voice that he'd been sleeping.

"Hello Marcus. Did I catch you asleep?"

He shifted his body, excited to hear her voice, and said, "I was lying here going over some documents. I must've dozed off for a moment. It's good to hear your voice; how are you?"

"I'm doing well. I sure could use a little company. Feel like coming over?"

"Of course. Is everything okay?" he asked. There were certain times when she calls when one of her cases weighed heavily on her mind but she rarely discussed them because she doesn't like bringing her work home.

"Yes, everything's fine."

"I'm on my way," he tells her.

"I'll see you soon." She ended her call. She was anticipating seeing him. He arrived at her home a little before she did and sat in his car waiting for her. Once she arrived and parked her car, he opened her car door and helped her with her belongings. He gave her a quick smooch. He walked inside with her. She placed her keys on the fireplace. He placed her bag on the side of the sofa. He turned to face her and gave her a comforting hug. She held him tight and pressed her face into his massive chest; she exhaled. His being there brought her comfort. She didn't like to admit it, but she needed him. She released her embrace and eased onto the sofa. Marcus often looked out for her, and she allowed him. He removed her shoes from her feet and helped her out of her clothes. He assisted her by lending his hand and gently pulled her to her feet. He kissed her lightly on the back of her neck, then her shoulder, and said, "Go and get a hot shower while I fix us something to drink." He gently smacked her on the ass. When he was allowed, he cooked for her and did certain chores she was too exhausted to do. She loved that about him. Although he was young, he knew what he wanted, and she knew that his demands were never selfish or ego-driven but were about her well-being. Part of her wanted him to find the love of his life, but the other she wanted him for herself.

While she showered, he went into the bedroom and noticed she'd left it a bit untidy, so he cleaned it and turned down the bed. He went into the kitchen and washed the few dishes she had left in the sink. Setting the ambiance for the evening, he turned down the lights and put on some soothing music. He lit two candles and then took out one of her favorite satin robes. By then, she had showered. He met her with a towel. Warm water was dripping from her exposed breasts. He kissed them both. He ran his tongue around her nipple and slightly pinched it with his lips. She was immediately aroused. He dried her body and then placed the robe on her. He went to the bedroom, got her drink, and handed it to her. She took a few sips.

"It's really great to see you, Marcus," she said. He smiled. He loved hearing that. He loved it when she needed him. He watched as she took a sip of her drink. Her deep, warm brown skin glowed from the candlelight. He wanted her, but not knowing the kind of day she had, he allowed her to take the lead. Perhaps she just wanted to be held, and there were many days when that was the case. She stepped towards him and kissed him. The kiss signaled what she wanted. She placed her arms around his neck. As he lifted her into his arms, sharing a heated kiss, she wrapped her legs around his waist. He walked over to the bed with her, and he gently laid her there. After sucking her breasts and kissing her belly, he began loving her body with his mouth until she was satisfied. He pushed her legs over her head which exposed her swollen clitoris.

He lovingly sucked and pulled on it while darting his tongue in and out of her. She gently pushed his head away while signaling she wanted him inside her. He gave her every inch of what she needed. He pumped her until her audible screams became silent. She used her strength to flip him on his back. He submitted. He could've easily overpowered her but allowed her to play at her leisure. He lay on his back, his member erect, standing at full attention as a soldier on the front line. She went down on him, sucking and taking him all in. His head throbbed with each stroke of her mouth on his dick. He almost lost his load immediately. This was her favorite moment. He tried hard to hold back, but her agenda was to cause him to release. He had no choice; she was begging him for it. Slurping his large cock, she begged, "Give it to me. Give me what I want baby, cum for me." In between sucking him, she ran her entire mouth up and down the side of his member. Flicking her tongue across his shaft, she placed it in her mouth and swallowed as much as she could. With him deep inside her warm throat, she swallowed to allow the muscles to create a sensation on his dick that caused him to finally let loose. It excited her, his hot cum erupting like lava from an active volcano. Not wanting to feel defeated, he quickly placed her on her belly. He pulled her hips towards him spreading her legs, he viciously fucked her. She wasn't intimidated. She welcomed it. With each thrust, he seemed to knock off all the stresses of her day. He hit her spot to the point her love juices ejected, lubricating his member. He was torn between drinking her sweetness and fucking her. He decided on both. He placed his hands under her and lifted her to his mouth. He sucked her from behind until she couldn't take any more. She released in his mouth. He mounted her and pinned her to the bed, forcing her to take all of him. She lay there with her face buried in the pillow, too weak to move. At that very moment, she reasoned within, "I may need to give this relationship thing another thought." However, as always, after the experience was over, she still felt he was too young for her, and he needed to find a younger mate more suitable for him. He lay beside her kissing her shoulder and rubbing her ass.

"Are you okay Jessica?" With her voice muffled, she answered,

"I'm more than okay. You always find a way to make me feel better." She rolled over and kissed him. Her heart melted. The emotions were there, she loved him deeply, but she would never allow the words to leave her lips. She kept them hidden inside for fear of leading him on. She longed to reveal her feelings to him, but for both their sakes, she decided against it. She climbed atop him and looked down at his handsome face. His flirty smile revealed his perfectly whitened teeth. His medium-brown eyes, which donned thick lashes, lit up as he lovingly gazed into her eyes. "Damn, he's fine as hell. I'm one lucky gal," she said while admiring his physique. She wanted to say it; she almost said the words, but instead, she closed her eyes, tilted her head back, and whispered so he couldn't hear her. "I fucking love you." Then she lowered her head and looked deep into his eyes while keeping her secret, a secret she's held for more than a year and a half.

"You are my Adonis."

"And you're my Aphrodite." She massaged his chest. He took both her hands and pulled her close to him. Kissing him, she passionately fed him her tongue. He readily received it. He was hard once again, and he slightly lifted her and inserted his penis inside. She was still wet. She bucked and moaned as she rode him. Hearing her love cries made him even more excited, his dick was much harder and stiffer than before. "She yelled baby are you ready?" He thrust his hips forward and whispered,

"Yes, baby I'm ready. Love me, Jessica. Love me like only you can baby. Feel us, Jessica, feel our love." With one final thrust of his hips, he gave her all of him. This action caused her to explode onto his throbbing member soaking him. She went limp. He held her. In an instant, she fell asleep. He held her body tight and did likewise.

CHAPTER EIGHT

Jessica was at the agency, leaning back in her chair and thinking about the intimate night she and Marcus shared. She smiled. Her mother was watching her.

"Why the big smile? What are you thinking about?"

She came to herself and said, "Oh, it's nothing, Mother," but she continued to smile.

"I know what it is. It's that handsome young Marcus."

"Oh, Mom, stop it."

"Oh, Mom, my eye. You know you love that boy, so why don't you go ahead and admit it? He's in love with you too."

"Why do you think I'm in love with him?"

"I don't just think it; I know you're in love with him. You'd have to be made of stone not to love someone after being in a relationship with them for two years. You no longer try to hide your relationship with him, and you two are always together. He makes you a better person. You're more pleasant and kinder after seeing him. You have this amazing glow."

"Mom, he's too young for me, and besides, he needs to find someone his age so he can marry and have children. I'm not interested in either one." Her mother took the cup of coffee she was drinking and walked over to Jessica's desk.

"Jessie, how is he ever going to find that younger woman if you're always with him? You know in your heart that's not what you really want to happen. How would you feel if he called you today and took you up on that offer? What would you say if he told you he found a younger woman he'd like to date?"

Jessica hated the way that sounded. She hated to admit it, but she would find the news a bit difficult to take. Her heart ached at the thought of him loving another woman the way he loved her. She forced a smile on her face, but her mother could clearly see that she was upset.

"See there, you don't like the thought of another woman with your man, do you?" She looked at her mom and smiled.

"Okay, Mother, it's true; I have strong feelings for him."

"Oh, I already knew that. You're the one who keeps lying to yourself. That young man adores you. Now, when are you going to tell him that you feel the same?" Jessica looked up at her mother as she sipped her coffee, waiting for her answer. She put her hand on her hip and asked her mother,

"When are *you* going to start dating since you've decided to be all up in my business?"

Her mom quickly responded, "Just as soon as I find someone who loves me just like Marcus loves you. I wouldn't have a problem with him being a younger man either. You have the best of both worlds. You have a handsome, fine young man who has his head on his shoulders, and on top of that, he loves you. You'd be surprised at all these older men out there who are so childish and don't have their lives together. They're still playing games like they're in their twenties. They're doping up on sex-enhancing drugs and all other sorts of pills and sleeping around with all these women. The dating pool is very thin when you get to be my age. I may have to get me a sexy young thing like you. Girl, I would proudly parade that young thing all around town for everybody to see."

"Mom, you're being a bad girl today." They both laughed.

They changed the subject to a case they were working on. A client's husband stole a family heirloom, and she hired Jessica to get it back. They also wanted to gain evidence of his infidelities to ensure a speedy, problem-free divorce.

"Jessie, you need to get Blaine here so he can conduct surveillance on Mrs. Harrelson's husband because I have a prior engagement. She's been calling all day. I wonder why she married the lowlife in the first place. He's stealing from her, and he won't keep a job. Perhaps she thought she could change him. She found him in the gutter, dressed him up, put him in a nice home, and gave him a job at her father's company, which he quit. Now she's stuck with a dressed-up lowlife bum and has us watching him so she can divorce him without him getting any of her money."

While looking through her files, Jessica said, "I don't care what they do; just as long as the checks keep clearing, I'll help her find anything. In the meantime, we still have other cases, including the Blaire Kensington case."

"How is that coming along? You haven't talked about it much lately."

"I'm still working on it. Perhaps we'll know something soon."

"I sure hope so. That family needs closure."

Jessica didn't want to say anything because she knew what she had done. She knew her mother would never approve.

She went out in the field to work on another one of her other cases. After the day, she returned to her office, closed it for the night, and went home. She was seriously thinking about what her mother said about Marcus. She couldn't stand the thought of Marcus being with another woman. She called his phone, but he didn't answer. For a brief moment, her mind wondered, "Had it already begun?" Her thought was interrupted by her cell phone ringing. It was Marcus. She exhaled and smiled.

"Hey babe."

"Hi Marcus."

"Sorry, I missed your call. I was in the bathroom."

"Oh, that's okay. I want to talk to you Marcus."

"Good or bad because I've had a hell of a day and need some good news."

"I'm not sure, but I would like for you to come over."

"I'm on my way; would you like for me to bring you anything?"

"I don't have anything to cook at the house, and it's a little late for a home-cooked meal. How about getting some Chinese food? Also, bring some of those garlic parmesan wings from that place you normally visit?"

"I got you, babe."

Jessica called her friend Blaine to see if he was on the stakeout for Mrs. Harrelson.

"Hey there, Coop."

"What's up, Jessie?"

"Just checking to see if you got your eyes open and your ears on."

"My eyes are open wide, and I have the subject in full view. I've been following him for the last fifteen minutes."

"Sounds great. Keep me posted. I'm heading home for the night."

"Okay, talk to you later; call me if you need me."

"Will do."

She made it home. Marcus hadn't made it yet. She went inside, showered, and put on something sexy. She picked a very short satin mini dress which revealed most of her breasts as well as her plump ass. She put her hair up in a ponytail. She lit aromatic candles and put on a little jazz. After fixing herself a glass of wine, she sat waiting. While she was almost certain of his love, she was hoping that what she had been preaching to him throughout the relationship had not taken root in his heart. She was ready to lay it all on the line. She was filled with nervous anticipation as she was now about to reveal her true feelings to the young man of which she shared her life and her bed over the past two years. She could hear Marcus' truck as he pulled into the driveway. She greeted him at the door with a kiss. She turned around and walked towards the kitchen. Putting on a performance for her audience, she dramatically swayed her hips from side to side, allowing him to admire her beautiful curvaceous frame. Staring at her ass, he was hypnotized as he watched it jiggle as she moved. He wanted to skip dinner and head straight for the bedroom. She knew he was watching and ensured the view was great. He set the food on the table and caught up with her. He embraced her and passionately kissed her with all his might. Things were getting heated quickly. She slightly pulled away.

"Later baby; let's eat dinner," she said.

"How about a little appetizer?" he asked. She kissed him and smiled while shaking her head, telling him no. He exhaled and reluctantly went to the cabinet to get some plates and eating utensils. He set the table, and she put the food on the plates.

"What would you like to drink?" she asked.

"I'll have a glass of wine, babe." She poured his wine, and they were seated at the dining room table.

"I've been thinking about you all day, Marcus. I couldn't seem to get you off my mind today."

"I think about you all the time."

"Marcus, how long have we been seeing each other?" Without hesitation, he said, "Two years and three months."

"Wow, you knew that?"

"You seemed surprised. I remember the day we met at the biker's charity event and the day you finally decided to see me. It took three months of me trying to convince you to go out with me. I remember our first time making love. If it has to do with you and me, then yes, I remember everything."

"You're so sweet. Marcus. You're such a good person. You've always been good to me. Your kindness is amazing. You've been more than patient and have managed to put up with me all this time."

"That's because I care about you and I know in your way, you care about me too. If you didn't, I wouldn't be here." They continued conversing. After dinner, they put on a movie and relaxed on the sofa. She snuggled her body comfortably in his arms. Curious about their earlier conversation, he asked, "Why all the talk earlier?"

"No reason." She turned around and faced him. She kissed him. "Marcus, I was thinking about us."

"What about us?"

"How would you feel if we were to make our relationship a bit more exclusive?"

"I thought we already were?"

"Well, yes, to some extent. I was talking about even more exclusivity. Would you like to take our relationship to the next stage?" He looked at her intently. Before he could answer, she said, "I'm not talking marriage or any-thing."

"Baby, I've been waiting to hear you say that for some time now. So, does that mean you're mine now?" She kissed him.

"Yes, that means *you're mine*. Marcus, I love you." She finally said it, and it felt great. He let the words he'd longed to hear soak in. He knew she meant them the moment she uttered them from her lips, and he was de-lighted.

"I love you too," he said, smiling. They discussed their love until heated desires took over. The night was theirs, and they enjoyed one another.

Not So Clear Cut

Jessica was awakened by her phone ringing, and it was Detective Armstrong. She quickly answered.

"Hey Jessica, we got the test results back from the cigar. She sat up in bed for a minute.

"Oh really; well, what's the news?"

"The test shows that the cigar is a match to Chadwick Lancaster. Where did you get it from?"

"I got it from Nigel. I took it myself."

"Are you sure it wasn't Chad's cigar?"

"Yes, I'm sure. Chad wasn't even there."

"You know identical twins share the same DNA, so perhaps that's what it is. I hear there's another more thorough testing that can be done to determine the difference between the two men."

"What about the fingerprints on the glass?"

"You won't believe this, but the only prints they got off the glass were yours. There were no other fingerprints on it. You must have given us your glass instead of Nigel Lancaster's."

"Oh fuck! Are you serious? Damn, how in the hell did I manage to screw up this bad. It was my only chance to get it. I can't believe I fucked that up. So, you said the DNA on the cigar matched Chad's."

"Yes, as I said, that's not uncommon in the case of identical twins. So, we have no case against Nigel. Unless we get those fingerprints or come up with something concrete, we have nothing at this time."

"Don't worry, I'll try again. I'll invite him down to the agency and get his prints that way. Just give me a little time."

"Okay, I'll talk with you later. We have another press conference. They'll be discussing the reward the family has in place for information. It's not a good look for us when we haven't been able to solve such a high-profile case. As you know, these things take time, and we don't want to rush into anything because whatever charges we bring against a suspect, we want them to stick."

"I understand. I'll do everything on my end." She ended the call. Looking down at Marcus, who was lying on his back, still asleep, she thought, "Damn, *he's so sexy*." She wanted him, but she allowed him to get his rest. She snuggled next to him and went back to sleep herself.

She was awakened by Marcus standing over her with a cup of coffee. He called her name. She opened her eyes. She could smell that he was already making breakfast for her. She'd slept so soundly that she hadn't noticed he was awake.

"Good morning, baby," she said, trying to get her eyes to focus. "What time is it?"

"It's close to ten o'clock." She sat up in bed.

"Don't you have to be at work today?"

"Yes. I still have time to go home and get dressed. Are you hungry? I made breakfast for us."

"Yes, I could eat a little something." He left and got their breakfast and brought it into the room. He sat next to her. "Why don't you bring a few of your things over so you won't have to drive back to the other side of town to get dressed when you're here? I think it would be more convenient for you."

"I can do that, babe. That sounds like a great idea."

"How would you feel about me giving you a door key?"

"If you're comfortable with that, then it's perfectly fine with me." "It's what I want," she said. He said, "So, there'll be no more of this nonsense speech about me finding a younger woman, right?"

She smiled and said, "If you even think about it, I may have to put a bullet in your ass. You're my man, and that's that."

He couldn't believe his world had changed for the better. Although he had marriage on his mind, he thought,

"One step at a time. If I continue to have patience, per-haps I can get her to the altar, but this will do for now."

After breakfast, Jessica went to the agency, where she watched the press conference on TV. She called Nigel. She asked if he'd be willing to talk to her about the case. He said yes, hoping to gain information from her and steering her in a direction away from him. He immediate-ly went down to the agency to speak with her. He walked in the door and gave her a quick hug, and then he took a seat. As always, she started with polite small talk before she got to the meat of the matter.

"How's the baby?"

"She's doing wonderful. She didn't sleep so well last night; she kept us both up until two in the morning. She's teething and has a slight fever, but her mom has gotten it down. You know she's good with that sort of thing. She's a great mother."

"So, you two have decided to make it work, I see."

"Yes, I figured it was time for me to turn over a new leaf. I'm a father now and want to do what's best for my daughter. I want to raise her myself."

"Is that why you decided to forgive Danielle for set-ting your home on fire?"

"Look, Jessie, I'd rather not discuss that. Besides, I told the police she didn't do it. I can't let the mother of my child rot in jail, especially since I was the one in the wrong."

"Well, that's mighty noble of you Nigel."

"Jessie, I know I haven't been a great guy; I mean, what can I say? I love women. I may have hurt a few in my day, but I didn't realize how much. I should've handled myself better than I did with Danielle. If I could take it all back, I would."

"You know Nigel, you can't lie to the police or commit perjury; that's illegal."

"Hey, it's up to them to prove she did it."

"Well, from what I hear, the evidence against her is pretty strong. They'll be going over her phone records to see where she was during that time. In fact, I hear they may be going over her records for the past two years." She fed him this information to alarm him. She wouldn't tell him they already looked them over. Not looking as confident as when he walked in, he leaned forward in his seat and asked,

"So Jessie, will they be able to tell everywhere she's been during that time frame?"

"Yes. According to the cell towers and her phone records, they can pinpoint her exact movements even if she wasn't on the phone during that time. You know they can do that for any phone. Your cell phone gives off a signal to the tower nearest the location you were. So, let's say if a person is in Arkansas, but they say they were in Miami, the phone records would show it." His mouth got dry. He asked for some water. She went to the fridge and got him a bottle of water. She handed it to him, confident that he would leave it behind when he left.

"What would it take for the police to get those records?"

"All they have to do is get a subpoena."

"What would they need to get a subpoena? Don't they have to have probable cause? They can't just go on suspicion, can they?"

"Well, in her case, they have probable cause, and they also have your statements against her to the police, so they're doing everything in their power to get that case solved for you. I even used my influence to have them speed up the case. I was concerned for you, and your parent's safety. I didn't want anything to happen to either of you, so they made it a priority to look for her. She managed to fall off the radar, and the trail went cold until you came back to Arkansas. When she was arrested, they were able to obtain her cell phone records legally. They're in the process of working on that now. Nigel, let me ask you a quick question, where were you when you first learned of Blaire's death?"

"I was in Miami. Mom called me."

"Were you ever in Arkansas during any time that week?" Remembering what she said about the phone records, he didn't want to outright lie, but he did.

"No; I don't think so. If I was here during that week, it would've been on business. I'd have to check my schedule. You know a lot has happened since then."

"Would you be willing to go down to the station to speak with detectives about the case? I want them to eliminate the family as possible suspects. It's normal procedure to do so."

"I wouldn't be of much help. I don't know anything. So, I would have to decline."

He was feeling the pressure of her questions. He was hoping to cast off any suspicion from him and gather information from her but instead, she turned the tables and managed to frighten him. He was nervous and at that moment, he no longer trusted her. He politely smiled as they made small talk as if neither of them was worried about the other. He announced he was leaving, claiming he had plans, and he left immediately. Jessica was disappointed when she noticed he'd chosen to take the bottle of water with him. She knew then that he had something to do with the murder, so she decided to up the ante. She requested her mother to make a lunch date with Nigel's mother and invite Danielle for a girl's day out. Again, she didn't reveal her plans to her mother, citing her life-long friendship with the twins' parents. Jessica wanted to speak with Danielle herself. She felt Danielle knew something and she possibly held the key that would crack the case. Her mother did as she requested.

Feeling validated, Danielle was excited to have lunch with Nigel's mother. In her heart, this legitimized the relationship between her and Nigel. Nigel was set to babysit so he made a day of taking the baby to the park. This would be his chance to prove he could be the perfect father he'd imagined himself to be. Nigel was holding the baby. Danielle looked at them both and asked, "Are you sure you're okay with keeping her today? You know she can be a handful at times."

"We'll be fine, baby; I got this."

"Are you sure because you've never kept her for more than an hour or so?"

"Yes, I'm sure. Now go on and enjoy your day with Mom."

She went to the Lancaster home. When she arrived, the women piled into one vehicle and left for lunch. Jessica knew where to meet them. She caught up with them and they ate lunch and explored the upper echelon areas of the city. Spaces frequented by the ultra-elite that only existed in Danielle's dreams. They were making small talk about the baby. Jessica looked at Danielle and said,

"Danielle, how would you like to go to this new baby boutique I've heard of? I saw an ad where they had some of the cutest little things for girls. I don't have any children myself, but I love buying things for friends who have children. Since I don't have any nieces or nephews, I just may have to spoil your baby girl." Danielle jumped at the opportunity.

"Mom, you and Mrs. Lancaster can go and do your thing while me and Danielle go and get a little shopping done. We'll meet you back at the house." Jessica and Danielle left, leaving the other two ladies at the restaurant. With the knowledge of Jessica's wealth, Danielle was impressed with her vehicle. She settled into her seat and relaxed. It was official. She had finally arrived. She was being celebrated by those she admired, and it was a long time coming. The years of turmoil she had endured at the hands of Nigel were finally paying off. When they made it to the boutique, Jessica allowed her to pick out what she wanted, and they left for another store. Once Jessica knew she was comfortable with her, she eased into the questions.

"Danielle, what are your plans for the future?"

"Well, Nigel and I plan to get married and raise our daughter together."

"So, you think Nigel is a good man?"

"In a way, I do."

Jessica said, "Really? I must say, I've known Nigel all my life, and he's always been the bad-boy type. Do you think he's changed his ways?"

"I think so. He seems dedicated to being a father and a mate for me."

They walked to a nearby bench, and Jessica said, "Danielle, sweetie, please have a seat. I want to speak with you truthfully." They both were seated. She faced Danielle and gently placed her hands on top of Danielle's.

"Honey, you and I both know Nigel hasn't changed. Now, I'm going to stop playing games with you, and I want you to hear me out for a minute. You don't have to say anything, just listen to me." Danielle looked a bit uncomfortable, but she nodded her head agreeing to listen. Jessica proceeded.

"I know you know something about Blaire Kensington's death. Let me tell you why I believe this. I believe Nigel killed her or at least he had something to do with her death. I believe Nigel was in Arkansas at the time of Blaire's death. I know for sure you were here based on your phone records. Your cell phone showed you were right in the area of the crime around the time it happened. It's a known fact that Chad was in Miami, so we know he didn't kill her.

I think you were still in love with Nigel, so you followed him to Miami. You rented an apartment there and that's a proven fact. You followed him back to Arkansas and to his brother's home. Then you followed him back to Miami. Now, we could say you two killed her together, or perhaps you had something to do with her murder.

Either way, I know you know something. I feel that Nigel is only using you and once he gets what he wants from you, he'll discard you. He's pretending to care about you. He's using this promise to marry you because he thinks a wife can't be forced to testify against her husband. He's buying your silence with a ring. Nigel will screw you over as he's done before and when he's purchased your silence, he will abandon you. Nigel will be arrested, and he will be convicted of this crime; it's only a matter of time especially when they're done analyzing all the CCTV data of the area and other evidence. If you cooperate with the police, the arson charges will be dropped against you, and you can claim that five-hundred-thousand-dollar reward the family has offered. It may be more. If you refuse to cooperate, you'll go to prison for arson. Eventually, Nigel will go to prison for murder, and who's going to take care of your beautiful baby girl?

Please don't throw her future away over your love for a man. Your daughter deserves better. So, what's your choice? You can assist the police and collect the financial reward. Then make a wonderful life for you and your daughter because, in the end, it's really about your baby. Are you willing to help, or will you go down with Nigel's sinking ship? There are a lot of good men out there looking for a beautiful young lady like you. You clearly deserve more than Nigel can offer. Don't fall prey to his lies. Blaire's family needs answers, and they deserve closure. They lost their only daughter, and his brother Chad, who's a good man, lost the love of his life due to his brother's selfish actions. Chad didn't deserve this. Did you know that Blaire was pregnant with Chad's baby? The man you're in love with, Nigel, stole that from them. What kind of man kills a woman and her unborn child? If Nigel can do such horrible things to his brother, what makes you think you'll be treated any better? Family means nothing to him."

Danielle said nothing, but Jessica could tell by her facial expression, that she was giving much thought to what she was saying. Her silence spoke volumes. She knew she'd hit her mark. She gave her a lingering and comforting hug. Danielle wanted to talk, but she kept quiet.

"Come on girlfriend, let's go," Jessica said. On their way back to the Lancaster home, Danielle rode in silence. She was thinking about everything Jessica told her. She thought about Nigel as well. She couldn't say anything at the moment. She looked out of the window, staring into space, not focusing on anything but her thoughts. If Nigel was going to prison anyway, what future did she really have with him? She didn't want to go to prison. The little time she spent in jail was difficult enough.

They finally arrived at the Lancaster home where Jessica pretended their conversation never happened. Danielle sat with Nigel's mother. Jessica left them and went back to work. Danielle was concerned about her daughter, so she thanked the ladies for a wonderful day, and she drove back to Nigel's place. When Danielle walked in the door, she noticed that Nigel had made it back with the baby. She didn't speak to him but instead, she went straight to Miracle's room. She noticed her sleeping. She was relieved. Nigel came into the nursery and stood behind her, looking over her shoulder. "We had a wonderful time today. She was a good little girl." He touched her shoulder. She moved just shy of his reach.

"Is everything alright?" Not looking at him, she said,

"Yes, why do you ask?"

"Because you're not talking much. You haven't said two words to me since you walked in the door."

Not wanting to alarm him, she shook off her thoughts and said, "I guess I'm just tired. I wanted to see my baby. I hate being away from her for any length of time."

"I understand," he said.

They went about their day as usual. Danielle continued to think about her future. She thought about Chad, Blaire, and their unborn baby, and then she thought of the role she played by keeping Nigel's secret. She knew she had to do something. It was only a matter of time before Nigel was arrested. Nigel had truly victimized everyone around him. She didn't want to be victimized a second time. The more she thought of his actions, the more repulsed she became by him. She was beginning to see things a lot clearer. She needed to make a decision, and she needed to make it quick, or she would soon be on the losing end again. She couldn't afford that, and her baby didn't deserve it. She wondered what purpose it would serve to have such a horrible guy in her daughter's life for the sake of having a father when he wasn't even a man of good moral character. But then again, he appeared to be trying to turn his life around. From her viewpoint, it was too little too late.

CHAPTER NINE

Danielle slept as close to the edge of the bed as possible. She didn't want Nigel touching her. Her mind was made up. She planned on leaving him. She got Miracle dressed, and she told Nigel she had errands to run. She left and went to the detective agency. When Jessica saw her walk through the door, she was pleased to see her. Danielle looked at Jessica, and tears began to flow.

"I need someone to talk to, and the only person I could think of was you." She offered her a seat, and she handed her a tissue.

"Can I get you something?" She shook her head. She sat there holding her baby while silently sobbing. She wanted to open up to her about everything she endured at the hands of Nigel. This was the very first time she would be able to tell anyone what really happened to her. She'd been too embarrassed to even mention to anyone else how big of a fool she felt for having fallen for Nigel. She didn't know where to begin.

"Take your time, sweetheart. I can only imagine what you've been through these past couple of years. All the things you did out of desperation, wanting to be loved only to be met with the selfishness of someone who didn't care about you." She couldn't believe that Jessica was spot on in her assessment of the situation. Danielle quickly nodded her head.

"Yes, you're right."

She told her all about Nigel's treatment of her after the death of her mother; the story of how and why she set his place on fire. After telling her entire story, Jessica's heart went out to her. Nigel had been very cruel to her, and she understood why Danielle felt she had no other recourse but to take the action she did. After all, she suffered at the hands of Nigel, it was a wonder *he* was still alive. She was angry for her. She was puzzled as to why she would move in with him and subject herself and her child to the possibility of more harm. After forming an almost sisterly bond, Danielle began to feel safe with her. Jessica gave her plenty of wise advice on dealing with men and emotional abuse. Danielle wanted to know how to go about telling the police everything she knew so that the arson and felony vandalism charges could be dropped against her. She just wanted to move on with her life. Jessica assured her that she was working on a parallel investigation and that she knew the detective involved in the case. She promised to take her to the police department whenever she was ready.

Nigel just so happened to ride by the agency. After seeing Danielle's vehicle there, he became alarmed. He passed by again and he saw Jessica walking Danielle to her vehicle. He hid out of their line of sight and called her cell phone. She looked at her phone and noticed it was him calling but she didn't answer.

She looked at Jessica and said, "That's him calling, what should I do?"

"Just play it cool and answer it. Don't tell him you're here. I want to help you and the baby to get out of his place and get you to a safe location and I'll be in touch." She gave Danielle a reassuring hug. Danielle answered her phone but panicked. She pretended to drop the call because she wasn't sure of what to tell Nigel.

She went to Nigel's place hoping to gather personal belongings that were important to her so she could leave. She was frantically trying to gather everything before he could come home. She'd hoped to be gone. As she was packing, Nigel walked into the apartment. He noticed her packing.

"What are you doing Danielle?" Startled by his presence, she put the things back in their place."

"I was getting a few things for me and Miracle. I'm taking her to Brinkley for the weekend. We'll be visiting family over there."

"Oh, okay. So, tell me, where did you go today? You left here without saying so much as good morning to me, and before I knew it, you were gone."

"I had a meeting with a friend?"

"That friend wouldn't happen to be Jessica Barnes, would it?" She nervously slammed the dresser drawer shut.

"Well since you asked, yes. She's a great person. She was at the luncheon with us yesterday and she and I got to know each other better. We went shopping and had a wonderful time. She bought our daughter some very nice things in addition to the gifts she purchased for the baby shower. How did you know I was there?"

"I just happened to ride by, and I saw your car over there."

"So, what, are you spying on me now?"

"No, I'm not spying on you. I told you I just happened to ride by, and I saw your vehicle. You didn't tell me she was at the luncheon yesterday."

"I didn't think it was worth mentioning."

"When one of Arkansas' best detectives is working a case that could potentially land me in prison, it's definitely worth mentioning. You don't know her as I do. That woman is Columbo in a skirt."

"Who's Columbo?"

"Oh, never mind that. She plays mind games with you. She loves to talk to you and bait you in and before you know it, you're confessing. She was one of the best female detectives in her field. Trust me, you need to stay away from her, or you're going to get us both caught up, and neither of us will be able to take care of our daughter. Is that what you want?" She looked at him and said,

"That's not going to happen. I'm not stupid." Not wanting to discuss Jessica anymore, she said, "I'm hungry. Can we go to lunch?" She had to throw him off with this. She needed to buy herself some time so she could make her move without any interference from him.

They went out to eat lunch. Nigel relaxed and had a few drinks.

"How many of those are you going to drink?" she asked.

"I'm okay," he said. "When the food gets here, I'll eat, and it'll absorb the alcohol, and by the time I leave here, I'll be good."

They continued to eat and drink. Nigel talked about going away on a trip with her and the baby. She allowed him to continue talking because she knew what her plans were. She simply agreed with him, nodding her head, all the while knowing she was leaving him. She played with the baby, finished her lunch and after Nigel was done eating, they left. As they were heading down Chenal Parkway, the baby began to get a little fussy. Nigel looked back at her for a brief moment and accidentally jumped a curb hitting a light pole. Neither of them was hurt but the police were immediately dispatched to the scene. Danielle and the baby were taken to the hospital as a precaution. Nigel refused treatment. The officer could smell alcohol on him. He gave him a breathalyzer test and found him to be over the legal limit for drinking. He was arrested and taken to the county jail. He was allowed a bond. His attorney bailed him out. He called Danielle but got no answer. His attorney drove him to his place. Once there, he noticed Danielle had been there and gone. She had taken her and the baby's things and left. He was disturbed. He gathered a few of his things, purchased an untraceable cell phone, took a large sum of money out of the bank, and went into hiding. He knew it was only a matter of time before a warrant would be issued for his arrest. He knew Danielle had double-crossed him.

During that time, Danielle had gone to the agency to speak with Jessica. Jessica called Detective Armstrong for a meeting. He listened to what Jessica had to offer him. He said if she could prove her case with evidence, they would make a deal with prosecutors, and charges against her would be dropped, and she would receive the reward money once Nigel was convicted. She agreed to tell them all she knew. When the day finally arrived, she turned over all the evidence she had to the police department. They immediately issued a warrant for Nigel's arrest when they saw the evidence. His fingerprints from his DUI arrest matched the print on Blaire's cell phone. Jessica asked for a chance to speak with the family before they went public with what they had.

She first told her mother, who was in shock. She then called Nigel's parents and informed them the police were looking for him. She called Chad as well. As his phone rang, she was very nervous about telling him. He answered, "Good afternoon, Chad."

"Hey, Jessie, what's up?"

"I'm afraid I have some news for you, and you're not going to like it."

"He took a seat and listened to her. "Have you spoken with your parents?"

"No, why? Is everything okay with them?"

"Yes, they'll be fine. What I want to discuss with you is that we think we may have found the person responsible for the death of your fiancée."

"Okay, who is it?"

"Chad, they have evidence and witness testimony that says your brother Nigel did it."

Chad was enraged. "Jessica, how dare you say something like that. Why are y'all harassing my family? Didn't I tell you that neither my brother nor I had anything to do with the death of Blaire? Had I known you guys were so incompetent, I never would've wasted my time coming to you. I could've done a better job of investigating this case myself."

Jessica allowed him to vent for a few minutes, and after hearing him out, she calmly said, "Chad, we have pictures and video proof. The police now have phone records proving that Nigel was here in Arkansas, not Miami. They've issued a warrant for his arrest. He's fled, and we can't find him. I want you to know the truth because when the news hits, you'll be bombarded by the media, and I didn't want you to be caught off guard. Can you come home to be with your parents? I think they need you."

Chad ended the call without saying another word. He needed proof that his brother had murdered Blaire. He wanted to know for himself. He called Amanda into his office.

"Yeah, boss; what is it?"

"Amanda, I need you to charter me a flight to Arkansas immediately.

"Sure."

He called Blaire's father and briefly spoke with him. The police told him they had a person of interest in mind, but they didn't tell him who it was just yet, and Chad didn't tell him either. They immediately flew into Little Rock. Chad went to his parents' home. His mother was in tears. His father was upset too, and he was trying to calm his wife. Annette Barnes and Jessica went to meet with the family as well. Blaire's parents went to the police station to get briefed. Eventually, Chad's parents were calm enough, and they went to the police station to speak with investigators.

They were placed in a large conference room along with Blaire's parents. All investigators involved in the case came inside. The detectives informed them of what they believed happened. After hearing all the facts, by the time the meeting was over, they had no doubt that Nigel was involved. They were asked to encourage him to turn himself in. Still stunned by the news, everyone sat quietly after the investigators left the room. Chad was broken-hearted. He loved his brother, but he was hurt at the thought that he would do something so cruel to someone so beautiful. He kept asking himself why he didn't see the signs. He thought about all the times his brother pretended to be in his corner while knowing what really happened. He went to Blaire's parents and apologized.

Her father said, "Chad, it's not your fault."

Mrs. Kensington was still trying to process the news. She couldn't speak. Chad's father continued to comfort his mother. Once the meeting was over, everyone went their separate ways. Blaire's parents went to their hotel room while Chad's parents went home. Chad went to his home. The police called a news conference. They informed the public that they were seeking the twin brother of Chad, and they blasted Nigel's picture everywhere. The news spread fast. Nigel was running out of places to hide, and he had to use a disguise when he went out.

The police had Danielle hidden in a safe location where Jessica often went to check on her and the baby. They wanted to keep her safe until after the trial. Jessica brought food to her and the baby, and she chatted for a while. They were getting closer, and the ladies got to know each other better. After visiting them, Jessica went to dinner with Marcus.

A few minutes after she left, there was a knock at the door. Thinking it was Jessica; Danielle opened the door without looking through the peephole. It was Nigel. He had been secretly following Jessica because he knew she would lead him straight to her. She was frightened to see him.

"Hello baby," he said, forcing his way inside. He tried kissing her on the cheek, but she turned her head slightly to avoid him. Unaware of his intentions, she was alarmed by his visit.

"What are you doing here Nigel? How did you find me?"

"Our friend Jessica led me straight to you. I've been following her for a few days now." Nigel was wearing a wig underneath his baseball cap. He was also wearing a fake mustache and large shades.

"What's up with that silly disguise you're wearing?"

"Well, sweetheart, I'm a wanted man thanks to you. I should've known you were going to turn me in; And to think I was falling in love with you. Where's my daughter?"

"Nigel, I don't think you need to be here. You should leave."

"I'm not leaving without you and my daughter. We're a family now, right? Isn't that what you wanted? Isn't that why you stalked me and blackmailed me? You're the one who wanted this. Now you're turning your back on me. No, we're going to be married." He walked up to her, kissed her lips, and then tried to kiss her neck. "Come on; let's take our baby and move to Mexico. We can go anywhere with the money I have. We could live out our lives on some exotic island, raise our baby together, and never look back."

"So, you want me and my baby to be fugitives. You must be crazy. I'm not leaving Arkansas. I'm afraid you're on your own. The best thing you can do for your daughter is to turn yourself in to the police."

"I'm not going to turn myself in. They're going to have to take me dead because I'm not going to go willingly. I can't do prison. I won't go, and I won't leave my daughter."

"You need to think of her safety."

"Look Danielle; let's get married."

"Why, so I won't have to testify against you? Well, it's too late. I've already turned over everything to the police. They offered me a deal and I took it. I took it because I love my baby more than I love a man. Remember when you were preaching to me about this very thing? Well, not only do I respect myself, but my daughter comes before any of this other bullshit. I'll receive the reward money, and they'll drop all charges against me, and I can raise our daughter in peace the right way."

"Well, what's going to happen to our daughter when you fall in love with the next guy? What if he decides he doesn't want to be with you? Are you going to follow him all over the country, stalking him and setting his shit on fire?"

"Nigel, it's not about me or you. It's about doing the right thing, so please turn yourself in. You've hurt enough people already, including your parents. Leave us alone. Don't drag your daughter into your madness. Besides, you never loved me; you only pretended to care. Why don't you do us all a favor and man up for once in your life and accept responsibility for your own actions."

"I don't want to leave my daughter."

"You have no choice in the matter." He looked at her with pitiful eyes and asked, "Well, can I at least say goodbye to her?" There was a long pause. She was reluctant but thought he would leave if she allowed the visit. He pleaded with her. She allowed him to spend a few minutes with the baby. He picked her up and talked to her. He kissed her, and then he held her close to his heart.

A loud knock at the door startled them both. It was the police. Nigel handed the baby to Danielle and demanded she go to the other room. In a panic, he pulled a revolver from his pocket. The police continued knocking. Nigel yelled through the door.

"Who is it?"

"Nigel Lancaster, this is the Little Rock Police Department; we have a warrant for your arrest."

"I haven't done anything wrong, so I'm not coming out. I have a gun, and I'm not afraid to use it. Now go away and leave me and my family alone." The police urged Nigel to give himself up peacefully. He refused, and he brought Danielle and the baby into the living room and forced her to sit on the sofa.

"Nigel, what are you doing?"

"Look, I can't go to jail. I'm sorry."

"Nigel, you're scaring me. You have a gun around the baby. Do you see what you're doing to your daughter? The police aren't going away. This isn't the movies. You won't get away. Have you ever known anyone to get away? You don't want to get into a standoff with the police. They always win. You're going to force their hand, and they'll possibly shoot tear gas in here and harm our daughter. You do know this won't end well." She continued pleading with him to give himself up peacefully.

"Miracle Lancaster still has a chance at a wonderful life Nigel, and you can give that to her. His heart softened when she called the baby's name. She pleaded with him to let them go. She stood up with the baby. She looked at him and said, "Are you going to do right by her?" She pushed Miracle to him and said, "She deserves that. She can carry on your legacy." He leaned over and kissed her. Danielle reached for the gun. He handed it to her, and she told him to say goodbye to Miracle.

"Now I'm going to allow the police to come in, okay? He nodded his head. She gave him one more minute with his daughter. She kissed his cheek and said, "Thank you, Nigel." She took the baby, and she opened the door for the police. They rushed past her and took Nigel into custody without further incident. Jessica, who was standing outside, came in to help Danielle and the baby. How did you know he was here?"

"I saw him tailing me. I wasn't sure if it was him, so I pretended to leave, but I parked around the corner and watched him come up to the door. By the time I was ready to apprehend him, he was already inside. I didn't think you were going to open the door for him."

"I'm sorry. I thought it was you coming right back. I thought you'd forgotten something. I opened the door without thinking."

"I'm glad the situation ended peacefully. Are you two okay?"

"We're fine. Thank you so much, Jessica."

Jessica walked them both to her car and drove them to the station for further questioning. Danielle saw Nigel in the back of the police car. He looked pitiful. Looking at him in the car, she couldn't believe how desperate she had been to be in a relationship with him. She was pleased with herself for turning him in. She sat in the car while Jessica got the baby's car seat and chatted with the police. Nigel continued looking her way. She pretended not to notice him and focused on her baby. Jessica finally came with the car seat, and they headed for the station.

Jessica said, "I'm so proud of you Danielle."

"I'm so grateful for all you've done for me and my daughter Jessica. You truly are a good woman. Instead of judging me, you helped me. I thank you for understanding my pain."

"I understand you because I know what type of person Nigel is."

"Well, you were right about him being selfish. I had to talk him down. He was willing to put our daughter in harm's way to save his own skin. He even had a gun. I was so afraid."

They went to the station, and she gave her statement. While she was giving her statement to the detectives, Jessica called Chad and his parents and told them the police had arrested Nigel. Chad rushed to the police station. He asked to speak with Nigel, who was in the interrogation room. He was allowed to see his brother. He walked into the room and saw him in handcuffs. Nigel looked up at his brother. Chad was the last person he wanted to see. He didn't want to face him, and he didn't want to be confronted by him at the time. He hadn't had a chance to figure out what he was going to say. He knew he couldn't simply talk his way out of this. He hung his head in shame. He heard Chad ask,

"So, is it true Bro? Please tell me it's not true. Please tell me you're not the man responsible for the death of my beloved and my unborn child. Please tell me the police have made a mistake."

"Chad, I can explain." With fire in his eyes and fury on his face, Chad moved closer to his brother. He leaned in and got directly in his face. His nostrils flared. His lips drew back into a snarl. With a roar in his voice, he said,

"You can explain? What in the hell do you mean you can explain? There's nothing to explain; did you kill Blaire?" By then, his parents and Blaire's parents were there, and they were allowed to watch through the glass partition. They wanted to speak with Nigel as well. They looked on as Chad continued to speak with Nigel.

"Answer me, damn it!" He demanded.

Nigel looked up at him and said, "Chad, you don't understand. I was in love with her."

"What the in the fuck did you say?"

"I tried telling you that, but you wouldn't listen. You insisted on keeping her for yourself. I didn't mean to hurt her. It was an accident. We were making love, and things got crazy."

Chad was beyond livid. With steaming eyes, Chad continued his fiery rage,

"You shut your mouth you lowdown, dirty, motherfucker. Are you kidding me? You killed my damn baby. You killed my wife-to-be. You stole my life you stole my world. You took my only reason for living and all you can say is you're sorry?"

"Chad, I didn't mean it, man. You have to understand that."

"I don't have to understand a damn thing. I understand you killed my child. After all I've done for you. I'm your brother. How could you do this to me?"

"I loved her too, Chad,"

Chad had heard enough. At this point, he wanted Nigel to quit talking. He was done hearing about him speaking of Blaire as if he loved her, especially since he violently murdered her. All he could see were images of Blaire being murdered. He remembered the horrid look on her face when he found her stiff, and motionless. Cold and naked, she was tossed aside like trash with a dead child in her womb. Before he knew it, he grabbed Nigel by the collar and slammed him to the floor. He straddled him and pummeled him in the face. Nigel pleaded with him to stop. "Did you stop when you were hurting my woman? Hell no, so I'm not going to stop beating your ass." The more Nigel talked; the more Chad tried to silence him by punching him in the mouth. At this moment, he felt as though he really could kill his brother. He continued to pound his fist into his jaw. He grabbed his throat so he could feel what it was like to be choked to death. With a firm grip, he squeezed his neck with both hands until the police came into the room and pulled him off of him. It took three large deputies to get him to release his grip. Nigel, who was a bloody mess, was helped up by another deputy. He was gagging for air. The deputies tried calming Chad as they understood his rage. After Nigel got his breath, he cried out to his brother.

"Chad, I didn't mean to man! I didn't mean it. I'm sorry. Let me explain!" Ignoring him, Chad turned to walk out with the deputies. Nigel screamed out loud, "Please don't leave me man. I need you!"

Chad turned to look at him and said, "I've had to save your selfish ass all of your life but this time you're on your own."

"Please don't leave me like this man. I'm your brother."

"I have no brother!" Chad stormed out as Nigel continued to plead with him.

Nigel was given medical attention. His parents came into the room. His mother went to him and asked him, "Son what have you done? How could you do this to your brother?" His father asked him, "Boy, how could you hurt your brother like this? You've hurt your mother, and that young lady's parents are suffering because of your actions. You've truly done it this time boy. To say we're disappointed in you would be an understatement."

Nigel tried to talk to his parents. Neither of them wanted to hear the excuses. His mother was hurt. She left the room in tears. Nigel was taken to a holding cell. As he walked out of the room, he saw Blaire's parents. Her mother was crying. Her father looked at him in anger. He was protected by the police and was rushed away.

The police called a press conference. The chief of police spoke with the media and let them know they'd made an arrest in the murder of Blaire. All gathered around and asked hundreds of questions for about twenty minutes.

Six months later

The trial was finally over, and Nigel was convicted of felonious sexual assault, and murder of Blaire Kensington, and the death of the unborn child. He ultimately received life in prison without parole.

All were satisfied with the verdict as they left the courtroom. Nigel's parents said their goodbyes to him. Chad walked out of the courtroom with Blaire's parents without saying anything to his brother. Jessica and Danielle were in the hallway of the courthouse.

"Danielle, I can't express it enough. I'm so proud of you. You really handled yourself well on the stand."

"Yeah, I was nervous after that defense attorney tried to pick me apart in there."

"You didn't crack, and you never wavered from the truth. Now you'll receive that reward money, and you can take care of that beautiful baby of yours. What are your plans?"

"I plan on moving back to my hometown of Brinkley and buying my mother's home and fixing it up. I'm thinking of possibly opening a small business, perhaps a daycare. I don't know yet, but we'll see. Jessica, I want to thank you for all you've done for us. I thank you for standing by me during all of this."

"No problem sweetheart. If you need me, give me a call."

"Okay, I will." They hugged, and Danielle left.

Jessica went to where Chad was standing as he conversed with the Kensingtons. He had his arm around Mrs. Kensington, comforting her. She was relieved that the trial was over. After conversing for a while, the Kensingtons, mentally exhausted due to all that had happened, returned to Miami.

Chad spent the next few months at Nigel's company, attending meetings and hiring more qualified candidates. He sent Danielle a monthly stipend for Miracle's expenses and set up a trust fund for her. Danielle would often travel to Little Rock to allow the grandparents to spend time with the baby.

Blaire's birthday was coming up, so Chad flew to Miami to set up a celebration and sail party in her honor. Each guest was asked to make a sizable donation to Blaire's Cancer Foundation, of which Chad served on the advisory board. With perfect weather, they enjoyed a small ceremony, and afterward, they set out from the shore. He renamed his vessel Blaire's Angel. In honor of his unborn child, without knowing the sex of the baby, whether boy or girl, Chad named the baby Addison. An image of an angel representing baby Addison was painted on the exterior of the vessel as well as the entrance. Blaire's parents were pleased with all he had done in honor of their daughter and their grandchild. They never once blamed Chad for her death, and they loved him as their own son. Blaire's family and friends came out to celebrate her life. Everyone entered the yacht and spent the weekend on the water laughing, enjoying fellowship, and remembering Blaire.

Karen Coleman is an Arkansas native. She enjoys writing exciting and dramatic stories. A phenomenal author with a distinctive style, she has demonstrated a sensational talent for steering her readers through every line and page with eager anticipation.

Karen has published several novels in various genres. Readers have described her novels as riveting, fast-paced, and thrilling.

Her teen novels are insightful and empowering. As a mentor who has worked with teens for many years, Karen understands the social challenges they face, and she skillfully addresses those topics with a finesse that lends excitement, adventure, and encouragement.

A self-proclaimed writer of fiction with an element of truth, Karen began penning her thoughts as a hobby. After many years of writing and encouragement from those around her, she began writing on a more intense level, eventually turning out several wonderful novels. She offers something for almost every reader, from her adult crime series to her teen books, there's something to be enjoyed by all. Her literary works have garnered much fanfare and have not only been enjoyed by her many readers; she's highly celebrated among her writing peers. Her books are meant to inspire, uplift, and entertain, leaving her audience asking for more.

Karen is also a playwright, actor, and former city council member. She's the mother of four and a Glam-ma of thirteen and counting. Her grandchildren affectionately call her Nana. She's also the proud mom of two rambunctious miniature schnauzers. When not writing or spoiling her grandbabies, she spends her time crafting, fishing, or enjoying a great barbecue.

Other Books by the Author

Arkansas Heat "A City Scorned"

Arkansas Heat "A Brutha's Obsession"

Arkansas Heat "Cindy's Revenge"

Arkansas Heat "Raising Delgado"

Arkansas Heat "Deceptive Practice"

Closer Than Enemies 1

Closer Than Enemies 2

Frozen Dreams

In the Wrong Game

No Place for Emily Ann

Metamorphosis "Good Girl Gone Bad"

Morgan's Path

Whatever Happened to I love you?

Be on the lookout for several more exciting projects.

Also check out the audio versions on Amazon, Audible.com, and iTunes

Special thanks to Professional consultants:

Ken Turner

Jerome Hobbs

Garland Camper